HARTSVILLE'S SEAL HEROES

The SEAL's Convenient Wife

The SEAL's Surprise Baby

The SEAL's Instant Family

The SEAL's Pregnant Roommate

The SEAL's Treatment

The SEAL's Hookup

The SEAL'S Convenient Wife

HARTSVILLE'S SEAL HEROES BOOK ONE

USA TODAY BESTSELLING AUTHOR

LESLIE NORTH

BLURB

When Navy SEAL Patrick Nelson returns from a black-ops mission, he's in for a shock—his six-year-old daughter Ellery has been abandoned by his ex and is currently in foster care. Now he has to prove he can be a good, stable father to Ellery, and that includes convincing Imogen Mendel, his daughter's gorgeous kindergarten teacher, that he's one of the good guys. Turns out, Imogen is more than just a pretty face. She's planning to testify against some dangerous people who are now threatening to silence her—for good. But not on Patrick's watch. He's got the perfect solution to keep Imogen safe and give Ellery a stable home: get engaged.

Imogen may have agreed to a fake relationship with Patrick, but she has to admit there's absolutely nothing fake about their attraction to one another. It's red hot and impossible to ignore. Before she knows it, they're turning into a real family and her heart is taking a painful turn toward falling in love. Things would be pretty good if not for the threats that escalate as the date of the trial looms closer. Thank goodness she has a sexy SEAL protecting her. But for how long? This fake marriage is turning far too real for both of them…

MAILING LIST

Thank you for reading "The SEAL's Convenient Wife"
(Hartsville's SEAL Heroes Book One)

Get SIX full-length novellas by USA Today best-selling author Leslie North for FREE! Over 548 pages of best-selling romance with a combined 2748 FIVE STAR REVIEWS!

Sign-up to her mailing list and get your FREE books:

www.leslienorthbooks.com/sign-up-for-free-books

CONTENTS

1

———

P atrick Nelson climbed the steps of the elementary school he'd attended as a kid. The front doors of the yellow brick building stood open to the spring weather, and he frowned. Weren't schools locked down these days? His hand automatically went for a sidearm that wasn't there, and then he gave himself a shake. This was the civilian world, where an unexpected open door meant nothing—and he didn't carry a gun in the civilian world. Well, not usually. And not to pick up his six-year-old daughter.

But he'd been on an extended deployment, and the transition back to life in his hometown was tough… especially since this mission had had more than its share of challenges. Moreover, he felt as if he'd let his responsibilities as a father slip—though not by choice. Yes, he'd been busy and out of touch, but his ex had made things ten times worse. Rachel had completely cut him off from any news of their daughter four months ago. Not one Skype session. No FaceTime. Nothing.

Patrick had been expecting Rachel to be difficult, after the fight they'd had before he left, but this was too much. Their arrangement had to change. He'd taken extended leave from the SEALs, and he was going to fight for full custody. He had no idea what that would look like… but he'd figure it out, because Ellery deserved better.

A man wearing a Hartsville Elementary T-shirt greeted Patrick just inside the front door. "Can I help you?"

"I'm looking for the kindergarten classroom," Patrick said, looking around. The building hadn't changed much since he'd been a student there, but it seemed strangely quiet for a place that housed kids.

"There are three. At the end of this corridor." The man pointed down the hall. "I think Ms. Mendel is the only teacher still here."

"It's only three o'clock," Patrick said with a glance at the oversized clock that hung nearby. "I thought school got out at three."

"Usually, but we had a field day, so the kids went home two hours ago."

Damn. He'd missed Ellery. Patrick had wanted to surprise her by picking her up from school—though he'd been nervous about it, too, since they'd had no recent contact. He didn't know Ellery as well as he should, and even when they'd been in touch, he'd often had no idea what to say to her. Despite that, he'd decided that he wanted to see her without Rachel around to interfere. Maybe the teacher could give him some insight.

"Thanks," he said and made his way toward the classrooms. The first room he looked in was empty, but in the next, a slim woman's figure was outlined against the bright light coming in through a wall of windows. "Ms. Mendel?"

She swung around, her hand going to her heart as if he'd startled her. "Hello," she said breathlessly. "I didn't hear you come in."

Was she the nervous type? That seemed at odds with teaching kindergarteners.

"I'm Ellery Nelson's dad. Is she in your class?"

"Oh, yes, she is," Ms. Mendel said, but her manner stiffened. "I understood that her father was out of the picture."

He held out his hands in a "look at me" gesture. "As you can see, I'm here. Do you need proof?" he asked, taking his military ID from his wallet. He walked closer to her. As he approached and the glare hiding her features receded, he could see she was a young woman with blonde hair. Pretty, very pretty, with delicate features and hazel eyes.

She scrutinized his identification card before handing it back. "Thank you, Mr. Nelson. So, what are you doing here?"

He arched an eyebrow at her. "I'm Ellery's father. I just got back to the States, and I want to see my daughter. I'm sorry you apparently received inaccurate information about my involvement in Ellery's life, but…"

She looked at him a moment and then seemed to relax a bit, though her expression was still guarded. "Why don't you have a seat?"

He looked around at the knee-high chairs and reluctantly folded his tall frame onto one. Maybe she just needed a little more information. "I've been deployed since not long after the school year started," he continued, "so I haven't been here for any events, but I was hoping to pick Ellery up. I didn't realize it was a short day. I guess I'll have to get in touch with her mother," he concluded, trying to keep the frustration from his voice. He wasn't looking forward to having to deal with Rachel, who'd probably do everything in her power to block him from seeing Ellery.

"So you don't know?" Ms. Mendel sat at the desk next to him, looking more sympathetic now.

"Know what?" He felt a prickle at the back of his neck, a sensation he'd learned to heed during his years in the service.

"I probably shouldn't tell you." She paused before seeming to come to a decision and continuing. "It's not really my place… but if I were you, I'd want to know. Ellery's been in foster care for the past two months. Her mother left her with a nanny and then, well, didn't come back. After more than a few days of not being able to reach the parent, the nanny called Child Protective Services."

"What?" Patrick shot to his feet and towered over the teacher. "Child Pro—does that mean foster care? Why didn't someone contact me? Where is she?"

"I can't disclose that." Ms. Mendel rose to her feet and took a step back, crossing her arms in front of her as if to ward him off. Her eyes strayed to her desk, where a phone sat.

"I'm her father," he said through gritted teeth as he searched for the control that had gotten him through so many tough spots. He had no wish to alarm Ms. Mendel. She wasn't the enemy. But she did know where his daughter was.

"I'm not disputing that, but you don't have custodial rights," she said. "You're not even on the list of people permitted to pick Ellery up."

"I'm not?" He and Rachel had talked about that when Ellery started school, and she'd assured him that she'd filled out the paperwork showing him as Ellery's father, with parental rights. Another lie. He shouldn't have been surprised.

"No. Look, I've told you as much as I can. If you want to see Ellery, you'll have to go through CPS. You should go now." Her words weren't an invitation, but a dismissal. He got that he was making her nervous, but he had to ask one more thing.

"Just tell me if she's okay," he said. Foster homes weren't always the best, and he wanted to know that his little girl was safe for now. "Please."

Ms. Mendel's face softened, making her look even younger. "She's struggling with this. Any child would, but I think she'll be okay in the long run. She's a resilient girl."

That helped. A little. But what he'd thought was going to be an unpleasant negotiation with his former girlfriend had just ramped up to a battle with an enemy that he knew little about—with Ellery's safety and happiness at stake. How the hell did he go about extracting his daughter from foster care?

"Thanks. I'll get out of your space now." He stalked to the door and made his way back to his SUV. Just as he was opening the door, his phone rang.

"Hey, man. Got plans tonight?" Anderson, one of his SEAL team members, was on the phone. They'd been buddies since high school.

"I could actually use your help right now, if you're available," Patrick said. Anderson was a strategist and might be a big help in dealing with the bureaucrats at children's services. "Can you meet me at the county office building?"

Anderson's reply was instant. "Of course, but why?"

"I'll explain when I see you." Patrick hung up and drove to the modern building located just outside town. In his head, he replayed the conversation with the teacher. She hadn't shared any information that was helpful beyond that last comment about Ellery's welfare, which he hadn't found all that reassuring. His job was clear, though: he had to get answers and formulate a plan to fix this.

Hours later, Patrick sat across the table from Anderson at one of their favorite hangouts, the Main Street Tavern. The beer was cold, the food good, and the atmosphere relaxing. All things that Patrick needed after wrangling with CPS.

"I thought there was red tape in the military," Anderson said, taking a drink from his beer. "That place could give a lesson in complicating what should be simple."

"You'd think being Ellery's dad—and wanting to take care of her instead of leaving her with strangers—would be the end of it. But apparently that means jack to them." Patrick traced the frogman-and-trident tattoo on his forearm that he'd gotten after his first SEAL mission.

The three different CPS representatives he'd spoken to had all asked the same questions while dodging his. Anderson had intervened more than once, getting more intel from them. His analytical mind sorted through the information more rapidly than Patrick's—and, of course, he wasn't hindered by the emotional responses that had made it difficult for Patrick to remain calm and professional. Anderson had even called the base to talk to a JAG officer to see how the Navy might help. Patrick knew he wasn't the only SEAL who'd faced a custody battle. Long deployments took a heavy toll on relationships. More than one of his teammates had returned home to find his wife and kids gone.

Once JAG got involved, the process had moved a little faster, giving him insight into what had happened and whether it was fixable. The answer to that was maybe, but it wouldn't be easy. Patrick just hoped he could get everything sorted out before Anderson's short leave was over and Patrick was on his own.

"I can't believe Rachel just took off," Anderson said after their cheeseburgers and fries arrived. "I mean, she was…"

"Go ahead. Say it. She was a piece of work." Patrick had no hesitation about finishing the sentence, but even he was surprised that Rachel had abandoned Ellery. He'd never thought she'd up and leave like she had. "She saw an opportunity and took it."

From what they'd pieced together, Rachel had become involved in a whirlwind romance with a wealthy guy who hadn't been interested in being tied down by a child, so Rachel left Ellery in the care of a hastily hired nanny. The nanny had thought Rachel was going out of town for a few days, but after a full week with no contact—and no payment—she'd driven Ellery to the police department and handed her over. She either hadn't known about Patrick or hadn't had any way to reach him. Patrick didn't want to think about his girl being dropped off like a lost wallet.

"I thought you two had worked something out," Anderson said after a few minutes of silence while they ate. "I mean, it's been years—it's not like this was a brand-new situation."

"Yeah, but she never wanted Ellery. Rachel was—is—a party girl with aspirations to land a guy with money. She and I were never meant to be serious." He and Rachel had never had more than a tenuous relationship after she discovered she was pregnant. Before that, they'd enjoyed casual sex and fun dates. Neither had wanted anything real or permanent, but he'd gotten her pregnant and he'd promised to support the child. And he had, handing over money whenever Rachel demanded it—which was often. He imagined she'd never been a great mom, but he hadn't expected anything like this.

"Right," Anderson said. "But that all happened years ago. What changed?" As his buddy and teammate, Anderson knew a lot of the history, but Patrick hadn't wanted to distract him with personal problems when they were on a dangerous mission.

"We had an epic fight right before my last deployment," Patrick admitted. "I mean epic. She screamed that she no longer wanted to be a mom. She hated the responsibility. She felt tied down."

"And you were stuck," Anderson said, nodding in understanding.

"Yeah. I mean, her timing couldn't have been worse—I had to report to base the next day." He sighed. "And then she cut me off. I didn't hear one damn word from her. No pictures, emails, nothing to let me know how Ellery was. I figured she was punishing me for not, I don't know, going AWOL and racing over to help her. But I never thought…"

"She put you in a hell of a spot. You should have said something, man. We'd have had your back."

"Nothing anybody could do while we were gone, but that's why I took the extended leave. I need to straighten this mess out and be a better dad. I'd been planning to fight Rachel for joint custody anyway. I was still trying to figure out what I'd do during deployments, but I wanted more say in my daughter's life." He'd known before Ellery was born that he'd never have a relationship with Rachel, and he hadn't wanted one. Ellery, though, deserved better than what she'd been getting with her father deployed so often and a mother whose first priority had always been herself.

"Anything I can do to help you, I will," Anderson said. "Can't imagine how much this sucks for you. I guess it proves the point that you should never trust a woman unless you're damn sure everything she says and does is true."

Patrick eyed Anderson, wondering about his friend's attitude. "There's that," he agreed after a minute, "but I think the lesson here is that—outside our SEAL team, anyway—you can't trust anyone with what's important to you. You have to take care of that yourself." Patrick had made a big mistake in that regard, and he had to acknowledge it. And now… now he was going to figure out how to fix it.

2

"What would you like to do with your dad?" Imogen asked Ellery. The little girl with ginger hair and blue eyes gave her a shy smile and a shrug.

This wasn't going to be easy, and Imogen wondered again how she'd ended up in the middle of this situation. Her principal, Ellery's foster parents, and the staff from Child Protective Services had all insisted that she was a crucial link. She could help father and daughter reunite while supervising the visitation and trying to objectively evaluate the relationship.

"Let's see. Your dad's in the Navy, right? Maybe you could make a ship out of construction paper together. I think I have a good pattern for that. Help me look." She took the girl to a bin stored on a shelf, and they sorted through various projects until they found one that would work. "How long has it been since you've seen your dad?" she asked gently as they located sheets of colored paper.

"Long time," Ellery said softly. "He wasn't here at Christmas."

Imogen knew from experience that the softness could shift to defiance in a heartbeat if Ellery was approached the wrong way. Imogen was beginning to understand how complicated the situation with Ellery's parents was, and her heart went out to the girl. She hoped something could be worked out with Patrick Nelson. She'd learned more about the man since their brief encounter earlier in the week. He was a SEAL who'd just returned from overseas.

She'd had a moment of fear when she'd told him Ellery was in foster care, a moment when she thought an explosion was possible, but he'd clamped down on his reaction. Apparently, he'd headed directly to CPS to sort it out. She had to give him credit for that. It didn't appear that he intended to be a deadbeat dad, although he had been an absent one.

She glanced out the window and saw Mr. Nelson crossing the lawn in front of the school. Imogen felt a fresh wave of nerves about her role in this. She had good reason not to get involved in anything messy. Her principal had promised to be around in case she needed support, since it was a Saturday afternoon and the building was mostly empty.

"I think he's here," she said to Ellery, and the girl's face instantly brightened. "Do you want to meet him at the door?" Without hesitation, Ellery skipped toward the classroom door. As soon as her father appeared and saw Ellery headed his way, he dropped to one knee and opened his arms. Ellery careered into him, throwing her arms around his neck and seeming to melt against him.

One question answered, Imogen thought, with a smile. There was a real connection between them. The love was obvious. They stayed that way for a long minute, which gave Imogen a chance to study the man. Earlier in the week, she'd noticed his dark good looks and height, especially when he'd sat on the little chair in her room. Any trace of defensiveness or anger was gone as he held his daughter. This was going to go better than Imogen had anticipated.

"We're going to make a ship," Ellery announced as she wriggled away from her father. She took his hand and led him to the workstation they'd set up with construction paper, scissors, glue, and crayons.

"It's good to see you again, Mr. Nelson," Imogen said when he looked at her.

"Call me Patrick." His face was serious, and maybe a little nervous. "Thanks for doing this."

"Imogen, then, and you're welcome," she said, giving him a little nod of acknowledgment before returning to her desk to grade papers and do lesson plans while father and daughter played. She was to stay in the room and observe but not interfere unless she felt it was necessary. She did have to suppress a giggle when Patrick contorted himself to get in the chair next to Ellery.

Over the next half hour, Imogen listened in on the conversation between them. They'd managed to cut out the ship while talking, but Patrick clearly didn't understand the purpose of crafting with a kindergartner. She shook her head as she heard him once again insist on a methodology for completing the project. He was focused on getting the task done and was missing the true reason for working together on it. He was supposed to be listening to his daughter. Ellery was trying to tell him about her foster parents' goldfish, the play the kindergarten had just put on for the school, and how she won the balloon toss at the field day. He was only half hearing his daughter's rambling stories. Imogen had to bite her lip not to say something. It was clear to her that while they might love each other, they hadn't spent much time interacting. That was a problem.

"Don't play with the glue," Patrick said for the third time. "I'll do that part." His voice had become more commanding with each repetition.

Wrong approach with Ellery, Imogen wanted to warn him, since he apparently hadn't figured that out.

"I want to," Ellery said, her tone becoming increasingly petulant.

"Do as you're told," he declared, as if speaking to a subordinate.

Uh-oh. Imogen looked up from her desk in time to see Ellery lunge for the open bottle of glue. The girl grabbed it, flinging glue across the desk, her father, and her own face. Ellery screamed as the glue got in her eye, and Imogen leaped up from her desk.

Patrick wrapped his arm around Ellery, automatically rocking her to comfort her as he wiped glue from her face with his fingertips. He'd been stunned by Ellery's rapid shift from sweetness to temper tantrum and now to wails and sobs.

"Here, try this." Imogen held out a wet wipe.

"Thanks," he said, trying to clean Ellery up without upsetting her more, but the girl still squeezed her left eye tight shut.

"Let me," the teacher said, kneeling at Ellery's other side. Without hesitation, Ellery transferred to her and allowed the teacher to gently open her eye and put drops in it. "Close your eyes now. It'll be better in a minute." Imogen held the girl so her head was tipped back, letting the drops work. Imogen gave him a small smile while she murmured soothing words to Ellery.

His daughter responded by burrowing closer into the teacher. Patrick sat back, feeling a little lost and a lot sad. He'd have liked Ellery to turn to him in such a situation, but he had to admit he'd never earned that from her. While he wanted to put all the blame on Rachel, he'd been part of the problem. He hadn't been around except for short stints. And even when he was stateside, he hadn't set up his place so he could bring Ellery there for long visits—and Rachel had never welcomed him into her home so he and Ellery might have had a chance to get comfortable with each other.

No. He was at fault here. He'd known what Rachel was like; it had been on him to control the factors he could control. He could have tried harder, pushed the issue, and known his daughter better. And the truth was that even now, if he got custody of Ellery, he'd still have to leave for extended periods. How the hell was he supposed to manage that? His daughter needed someone like Imogen, who appeared to instinctively know how to care for a child. Someone Ellery could turn to when she needed comfort.

"Better?" Imogen asked, looking down at Ellery's face. "Open your eyes, pumpkin."

Ellery's eyes popped open, and she grinned up at Imogen. "I'm not a pumpkin."

"Are you sure?" Imogen teased the girl. "How about an apple?" Ellery shook her head. "A green bean?"

"Yuck," Ellery declared, wrinkling her freckled nose. "I don't like those."

"You'll learn to when you're bigger, but you know what we have to learn first." Imogen put the girl on her feet, flicking away a glob of glue that clung to her shirt.

"Nope." Ellery shook her head.

"I think you do." Imogen gestured to the mess across the tabletop and on the floor. "What's rule number one in Ms. Mendel's class?"

"Clean up your mess," Ellery chanted.

"That's right," Imogen said. "And as a special Saturday treat, your dad and I will help. Go get the trash can from over by the door, please."

Ellery skipped toward the door with no argument, making Patrick wonder again at the ease with which the teacher managed the child. Was she some kind of miracle worker? He studied her, wondering if he could imitate her behavior.

"Here's a note," Ellery said from the door as she scooped up a white envelope. Without ceremony, she ripped it open and pulled out a sheet of paper.

"Ellery," he warned. "I'm sure that's not for you. You don't open other people's things." For a moment, he thought his daughter was going to stick her tongue out at him. Her face was pure belligerence. Instead, she gave him a haughty look and delivered the paper and envelope to Imogen.

"Here you go," Ellery said in a sweet-as-pie voice.

"Thank you for bringing this to me, but your dad is right." Imogen flipped the envelope over and showed it to the girl. "See? This has my name on it. M-E-N-D-E-L."

"There's no Ms.," Ellery argued.

"Well, sometimes people forget that part," Imogen explained. "Go help your dad clean up. I'll be there in a minute."

While Ellery headed back to get the trash can, he couldn't help watching Imogen. She truly was amazing with kids, and she was far prettier than he remembered any kindergarten teacher being. That thought fled his mind when he saw her expression as she scanned the note. She turned pale, and her hand covered her mouth as if holding in a scream.

"Something wrong?" he asked, sensing a threat. Out of habit he did a quick scan of the room, checking outside through the windows, but he saw no apparent danger except for whatever was in that note.

"What?" Her voice was distant, as if coming from deep inside her.

"The note," he insisted. "Is it bad news?"

She gave herself a little shake. "No, just… um… unexpected is all. Let me just…" She carefully folded the note and walked to her desk, where she opened a drawer and stuffed the note into it. For a second, she kept her focus down and rested her hand on her stomach like she was going to be sick. Then she lifted her head, her hazel eyes meeting his, and one thing was clear. All the life and vitality had gone out of her. What the hell did that note say?

"Recycle?" Ellery's question echoed loud in the quiet classroom. She held up two different bins.

"Yes, that's fine," Imogen said, finding a smile for the girl, "since it's mostly paper." Imogen returned to his side and acted as if everything was fine. He didn't have the right to question her further, as much as he wanted to. But she'd been kind to him, and he wanted to repay her if he could. Even if this was no time for him to take on someone else's problems. He had plenty of his own.

3

Patrick drove home, unlocked the front door, and dropped his keys in the tray in the entry. He loved this little house that he'd inherited from his grandmother. It was more of a cottage, with three small bedrooms upstairs and living space down. The location, though, was the winner. It was at the end of a lane, with woods nearby for country walks.

As a kid, he'd explored those woods and tromped mud into the house. He could almost hear his grandmother's voice scolding him gently. Sometimes he thought he caught the scent of the gingersnaps she'd made just for him. Slowly, he'd been making the place his home, but remnants of his grandmother remained, such as the lace curtains on the long windows and the rooster-themed decorations in the kitchen. He'd always felt welcome there, felt like he was part of a family.

Except now. He felt empty without Ellery, to a point that surprised him. Sure, he loved her—she was his daughter. But he'd never really focused on what that meant. He'd never thought about what he was taking from both of them by going on with his life for the most part as if she didn't exist. She'd only ever been in this house for an occasional overnight stay while he was on leave. Those occasions had been few—and that was on him; he hadn't made any effort to change the situation—giving them little opportunity to truly get to know each other. That failing had been obvious in Imogen's classroom, and he regretted every missed chance to be with Ellery. He had so much to make up for if CPS let him.

A car door slamming in the driveway caught his attention, and he drew the curtain back. With a grin, he stepped onto the porch to welcome his brother, who'd texted earlier to suggest having dinner together. Todd leaped up the steps and gave him a bear hug, slapping him hard on the back.

"God, it's good to see you," Todd said when the hug ended.

"Same," Patrick responded, feeling more emotional than he usually did. He and Todd were closer than most brothers, a product of their upbringing. They rarely spoke of their mother, who'd abandoned the family when Patrick was eight, and Todd only two. She'd died shortly after she left. That experience had made their bond tight, with Patrick taking on extra responsibility for his younger brother. Their dad had been a good man, doing the best he could by his sons, but he too had died young. Five years now. It seemed like forever.

"I've got pizza and beer in the car," Todd said. "Let's eat on the porch." He headed back to his car, opening the rear door and pulling out a pizza box and a six-pack.

"Beer? Shouldn't you be studying for finals?" Todd was a few weeks from graduating college with a degree in communications.

"Love you too, bro." Todd grinned at him, giving his usual response when Patrick tried to tell him what to do. Todd placed the pizza box and beer on the table between the porch rockers. "Sit down and relax."

Patrick sat, knowing it was pointless to try to resist his brother's attempts to care for him. Sometime in the past few years, Todd had grown up and decided he needed to help Patrick the way Patrick had helped him when they were younger. The problem was, Patrick wasn't good at being mother-henned.

"It's so awesome here." Todd sat in a rocker and propped his feet on the railing before cracking open a beer.

"You're always welcome, except when you've got studying to do." Patrick shot him a look and reached for a slice of pizza.

"Relax," Todd said, chugging half his beer. "My classes are going great. I have two exams and one project to complete, and then I'm home free. You're coming to graduation, right?"

"Wouldn't miss it." Patrick resisted the urge to nag Todd about his schoolwork. It was second nature to look out for him, but he knew there was nothing to worry about, since Todd made the dean's list every semester. "Any job prospects?"

"A couple. I had an interview with Alden Electronics. They have a PR position open that would be a good fit for me, I think. And I've got another interview next week with the hospital for assistant director of their community outreach program."

"Both local? Are you looking elsewhere?" Patrick asked, worried that Todd had too limited of a scope.

"A little," Todd said, "but I don't know about moving."

"This is the time to go see the world, little brother. Get out of Hartsville," Patrick said, reminding himself that his experiences had been very different from his brother's. He'd gone straight from high school to the Naval Academy to SEAL training. After which he'd been to the corners of the globe, which he enjoyed—even if he wasn't seeing the usual tourist attractions.

Todd chuckled. "That's you. Not me. I like it here. Small-town life suits me, and I'm more of a homebody than you are."

"Think about it," Patrick encouraged. "It doesn't have to be permanent; you can always come back. But you should try living in a big city or a different part of the country." Patrick hoped Todd's reasons for wanting to stay in the area were genuine and not attached to a sense of responsibility to him. He didn't need anyone looking out for him.

They ate and chatted, Todd catching him up on local news and what was going on with shared acquaintances. Patrick gave his brother a cleaned-up, declassified version of what had been a shitshow of a mission. When the sun started to sink toward the horizon and the pizza was almost gone, Todd changed the subject to the one that Patrick had been avoiding. He knew Todd had probably wanted all the details as soon as he arrived, but he'd let Patrick eat first. One more example of Todd trying to be the caretaker.

"I'm so sorry about Ellery," Todd said. "I had no idea what was happening with her. Poor kid."

"Not your fault," Patrick said. Even if someone from the local police department or CPS had connected with Todd about Ellery, he'd have had no legal right to claim her. Just another thing Patrick had mismanaged when it came to his daughter.

"Maybe, but I was only an hour away. I could have helped her or at least tried to get a message through to you."

"I doubt you'd have been able to reach me, and you had your classes to manage. You couldn't be responsible for a six-year-old." Patrick didn't want Todd beating himself up over this.

"She's one of the few people in the world I'm related to. I'd have done anything for her," Todd said, reminding Patrick that perhaps his brother had a better grasp on family than he did. He'd shirked his parental responsibilities until the situation had hit a breaking point.

"You can help us both now by completing the mountain of paperwork CPS requires. You and Anderson are my character references, so I'm sorry to say they're probably going to crawl through your background as well as mine."

"They won't find anything objectionable other than a few speeding tickets," Todd said. "What happens after that?"

"The team from CPS assesses everything about me and Ellery starting Monday. They'll check my service record and talk to my commanding officer. I have to see a psychologist for an evaluation, and so does Ellery. And if all that goes well, I've got a shot at custody."

"Sounds like a pain in the ass," Todd said, "but it'll be worth it in the end."

"That's my takeaway, too." He tried to sound calm, but he wanted this process over and done with so he could bring Ellery home and start building a relationship with her.

"How'd today's visitation go?" Todd asked. Patrick was surprised that it had taken his brother so long to get around to that question.

"All right, I think. We met in Ellery's kindergarten classroom with the teacher as our supervisor. We tried to make a ship out of paper and really just made a mess. She's grown so much since I saw her last." Ellery must have added three inches in the past six months, and there was something about her attitude that was different. Maybe a little hardened by her experiences, sadly.

"I'll bet." Todd opened another beer and took the last piece of pizza. "Last time I saw her was August, right before your deployment.

Pretty soon, she's not going to be a little squirt anymore. You ready for that?"

Was he? Raising a child, a daughter, was going to come with challenges. But he'd faced those before. "It's going to be tough. I don't know much about being a dad." Overall, he was optimistic about it, but he could admit his worry to Todd. Patrick thought about how easily Imogen had managed those moments when Ellery threatened to go off the rails. Imogen had known when to cajole and when to command. He'd gone straight for command, resulting in glue and paper everywhere. It'd be funny if it weren't indicative of the uphill battle ahead of him.

"You'll get the hang of it," his brother said. "Never seen you fail at anything."

"Maybe, but I'm not a natural at this. Imogen is."

"Who?" The shadows were lengthening, but Patrick could make out the curious expression on Todd's face.

"Imogen Mendel, Ellery's teacher."

"I know her!" Todd's smile was instant. "We work at the community food bank together, every other Saturday. I wish I'd known Ellery was in her class. I could've kept tabs on my niece." Patrick wasn't surprised that Imogen would volunteer at a food bank. She seemed like a giving person. "She's awesome. Hot, too."

"She is that." Patrick hadn't let himself focus on that, given the circumstances, but Imogen was a combination of hot and nice that he hadn't often found. If he weren't in the middle of a custody battle that she, too, was playing a role in, he'd have asked her out. As it was, he hoped to have her as an ally with CPS. They seemed to trust her judgment and assessment of the situation. "I'm glad Ellery has someone in her life she can trust."

"It'll be you soon enough," Todd said, "but it won't hurt for her to have support elsewhere. And Imogen is a good egg. She's nice to everyone. I've seen her sweet-talk the most difficult people. It never takes her long to get folks on her side."

"Do you know anything else about her?" Patrick asked casually. He thought about the note he'd seen her crumple and put in her desk drawer. Someone was definitely not on her side, by her reaction to the letter. He was tempted to probe, see if Todd knew anything about a problem that Imogen might have or details of her background. But he stopped himself. It was none of his business, and he didn't think she'd appreciate being a subject of discussion. Imogen had a secret, though. He was sure of that.

"Not really. Nice, pretty, caring, punctual," Todd responded. "That about sums up my knowledge of her. As far as I know, she doesn't have any flaws."

Patrick had learned long ago that everyone had flaws, but he wondered if Imogen's were of her own making.

4

Imogen filed into the conference room with the representatives from Child Protective Services and took her seat at the table. This wasn't her norm at all. Only once before in her career had she been asked to sit on such a panel, and she hadn't liked it. It was uncomfortable for anyone except the most coldhearted individuals to decide the fate of a child or a family. There were a thousand considerations to be taken into account.

The birth parents were usually the best choice in most cases. Except when a mother had abandoned her child. Imogen grimaced. How could any woman do that? She couldn't even imagine. It was painful enough for her to part with her kindergarteners on the last day of school before summer break. Patrick seemed committed to Ellery despite his previous absence, so that along with his blood ties were two things going for him. He loved his daughter, that had been obvious, but…

But he didn't seem to understand Ellery's nature—or any child's nature, for that matter. And Ellery was special. She was a glittery ball of energy, always zipping about, but she crashed to the ground as often as she sailed through the air. Those were the tough moments with her. At the beginning of the school year, Imogen had noted some trust issues. When Ellery was put in foster care, those issues intensified, along with some behavioral problems. Imogen's classes in child psychology told her that Ellery's challenges were due to the circumstances, but that didn't make them any easier to manage.

Imogen smoothed out the agenda in front of her that listed all the individuals and agencies involved in the day's hearing. A slight rustle at the door had her looking up. Patrick Nelson walked in, dressed in a nicely fitted dark suit, accompanied by another man who wore a naval uniform. The newcomer was introduced as a JAG attorney, Patrick's legal representation provided by the Navy.

Imogen's attention remained focused on Patrick, and she wondered why he wasn't in uniform, too. She hadn't realized until after he'd left her classroom on Saturday that he was Todd's brother. She should have; they looked alike, though Patrick was a harder, more haunted version of his younger brother. Todd was lighthearted and jovial, always quick with a laugh. Patrick was tough, taciturn, and far, far sexier.

She gave her head a shake and straightened the pencil alongside her agenda. She had no business thinking about how sexy the father of one of her students was. Terribly inappropriate, and besides, she wasn't interested in a relationship. She couldn't be, not with her own situation. Even being in what was technically a legal meeting made her nervous. Could she get in trouble for participating in this process under an assumed name? Or could the appearance somehow jeopardize her protected status?

She swallowed hard, trying not to think about the threatening note and phone calls she'd received lately. That wasn't supposed to happen, but it had. Adding frustration to her fear, her handler in the program didn't seem concerned. He told her to be cautious and wait, since the trial wasn't far off. Just a little longer, he kept saying. She feared the threats would get even more intense as the trial approached.

All the more reason for her not to draw attention to herself today. She'd speak when asked a direct question, and other than that, she'd keep her thoughts to herself.

"Now that everyone's here, let's get started," Anita Hamilton, the lead representative from CPS, said. "I want to start by reviewing how Ellery came to be in foster care, and then we'll move on to a discussion of whether or not Mr. Nelson will be granted custody of his daughter. On March…" She read from a report, stopping periodically to confirm details with others at the table. "According to records at Hartsville Elementary School and the reports of her foster family, Ellery has experienced tantrums and episodes of defiance since her transition into foster care."

Imogen cringed a little at the reference to school records. She'd been able to manage Ellery's behavior in her classroom, but the music teacher and the recess monitor had both had incidents with Ellery that resulted in the girl going to the principal's office. All of that was documented in the notes and undeniable.

"Ms. Mendel," Anita continued, turning to Imogen, "can you verify these reports from your experience?"

"Those incidents did occur, but Ellery is, in many ways, a typical child of her age group," Imogen said, having prepared these remarks in advance. "Her mood can be changeable, and she sometimes dislikes being told what to do, which isn't unusual among children as they transition to the structure of school for the first time."

"Would you say that her behavior worsened after her mother's disappearance?" Anita asked, and it seemed as though everyone around the table leaned in, waiting for Imogen's answer.

Imogen hesitated. She wanted Patrick to get custody of his daughter —and in her heart, she thought that was best for the child—but she had some reservations. Did Patrick have the tools to navigate parenting a difficult, highly strung child who might face some mental health issues as a result of her experiences? Imogen wasn't sure, so she chose her words carefully.

"I've seen some changes. Nothing dramatic," she qualified, "but I would have to answer yes, to a certain extent." There had been one spectacular temper tantrum a month ago over a simple request to take her place in line. Fortunately, only Imogen and one other teacher had witnessed it. Imogen had been able to defuse the situation quickly without involving the principal or the school counselor. She had reported it to the foster mother when the woman came to pick up Ellery that day.

"And having observed Mr. Nelson with his daughter, do you think he is fit to father Ellery?" Anita pressed, making Imogen feel the pressure of all eyes on her.

"I believe that Mr. Nelson loves his daughter and has the best intentions when he seeks custody." There, she'd said what was true without elaborating.

"I sense a *but* in your statement," another member of the CPS team said. "Would you explain further?"

Dang it.

"As I understand it, Mr. Nelson has never been a full-time father to his daughter. There'll be a learning curve, as there is in any parenting situation. He's just coming to it a little later than most. Again, let me repeat, the love already between them is a good foundation for developing a stronger bond." She hoped her honest reply didn't damage Patrick's chances of getting Ellery, but she couldn't lie to this panel.

From there the discussion moved on to how Patrick would manage childcare when he was deployed on SEAL missions. Patrick insisted that he could find a quality nanny to provide live-in care when he was gone. To strengthen the argument, the JAG officer brought forth documentary evidence stating that others in similar positions managed, and there was no evidence to suppose that Patrick would not.

Much of the panel remained unconvinced, though, and the discussion stretched on, going nowhere for several minutes as people expressed their views. Most were reluctant to openly insult Patrick and question his level of allegiance to his daughter, since he was a decorated SEAL and had clearly served his country, but the doubts remained thick in the air of the conference room. The discussion devolved into other issues, including what would happen if Patrick were killed in the line of duty. Where would Ellery go then? The JAG officer objected to this line of thought, stating that all members of Special Forces were required to make arrangements for dependents and that would be dutifully done. Patrick's brother, Todd, was mentioned as a potential guardian.

Just when it looked like the meeting would move on, another question was raised about how Patrick would be contacted should something happen to Ellery while he was deployed. Once again, the JAG officer assured the room that the Navy always had the ability to communicate with its units should the situation be truly life and death. The response didn't satisfy everyone in the room, but Anita attempted to move the discussion along.

Imogen glanced at the clock. They were more than two hours into the meeting, the room was becoming stuffy, and she increasingly disliked her role in the entire mess. They were circling back to Ellery's mother's abandonment when a woman from CPS who had been the most negative spoke again.

"I do wonder," she said, "where all the fatherly love Ms. Mendel feels you possess, Mr. Nelson, was when Ellery was being placed in foster care in the first place. What does that say about you?"

Imogen bridled at the unfairness of the question, since Patrick had been deployed and completely unaware of the situation. She'd kept her mouth shut for the past hour, but her restraint finally failed her. Ignoring her pledge to stay in her lane and not bring undue attention to herself, she cleared her throat and addressed the other woman.

"Mr. Nelson had no knowledge of what Ellery's mother was doing. How could he have?" She looked around the room, daring anyone to answer. "I'm sure, had he been informed at the time, he would have intervened and prevented his daughter from entering the foster system. Let's keep in mind who the person really at fault in this situation is. Ellery's mother abandoned her in the care of a nanny, leaving no money and no contact information—for herself or for Mr. Nelson."

Everyone was focused on her again, a sensation she'd never liked and did even less in this situation. It made her feel as though she were on trial, and she pushed down her fear of being a witness and having to withstand cross-examination. That would happen soon enough.

"Ms. Mendel is correct in her assessment," the JAG officer said. "Captain Nelson is not at fault and could not have predicted or controlled the actions of his child's mother. That is not a reasonable line of inquiry." The officer's steely voice and firm tone put an end to the discussion, and a minute later, he and Patrick were asked to leave the room so the others could confer and arrive at a decision.

Imogen rose from her chair, planning to follow them out, but Anita stopped her. "You're part of this decision as well. If you're unfamiliar with the process, we don't vote. We discuss the case until we can find common ground."

Imogen settled back in her seat, determined to say as little as possible. A few of the voices were fairly strong against Patrick gaining custody, but most took a more moderate approach. After an hour, consensus was reached, and Patrick was invited back into the room.

As he entered, he looked around, his gaze falling on Imogen for a half second longer than it did on the others. Had he counted on her to speak on his behalf? She'd done what she could, but she understood some of the reservations others held.

"Mr. Nelson," Anita began when everyone was seated, "you are being granted *conditional* custody of Ellery. You will be subject to review by this panel at three-month intervals and should be prepared for drop-in visits by a CPS representative. You also must make childcare arrangements for Ellery for when you are on active duty, and those arrangements must meet with our approval. A formal plan for that must be submitted and approved in advance of any deployments, or custody will be revoked."

Patrick's face hardened, but he said nothing, only dipping his chin in acknowledgment. Imogen felt sorry for him. He must have been hoping to get custody, free and clear.

"Furthermore, we strongly suggest you convince the mother to legally relinquish any claim to custody of Ellery. Without that, she could come back and challenge this decision. It's unlikely, considering her actions, that she'd receive access to her daughter, but it would cause a major disruption in your life and Ellery's. Your counsel can advise you how to proceed in that area. Do you have any questions?"

"When can I get Ellery?"

"You may pick her up at the foster home Saturday morning," Anita said. "I trust the bedroom in your home is ready for her and that you have an appropriate car seat."

"I do," Patrick said. The panel had discussed his home, even viewing pictures of it. That was one point about which no one had argued. "How long will custody be conditional?"

"We'll review it, as I said, every three months. If you can prove that Ellery is doing well under your care and you meet the other conditions, we will consider permanent custody at a later date."

The JAG officer put his hand on Patrick's arm as if to stave off any negative reaction. But Patrick merely stood, nodded at the people seated around the table, and went out. Imogen gathered her things and followed. She passed by Patrick in the hall talking to the JAG officer.

"I can't believe this. She's my daughter," Patrick was saying as Imogen went by.

"That's how these things go," the other man said. "It could have been a lot worse."

"Maybe," Patrick said, and Imogen felt his eyes following her until she turned the corner.

5

———

Patrick propped his feet on the porch rail and balanced a plate of cheese, grapes, and crackers on his lap. The day hadn't gone as he'd planned. Despite the JAG officer's warnings, he'd hoped to be granted full custody with no conditions attached and have Ellery with him immediately. He'd had to bite his tongue several times as the members of the panel expressed their opinions to the contrary.

Talking to Todd as he drove home had helped calm him. He was getting his daughter, just not how he wanted to. At least, for now.

He looked down the lane toward the woods. He loved living there, on the edge of the forest, where it was peaceful and safe. Great place to raise a kid. He'd run wild there when it was his grandmother's house, and he wanted the same for Ellery. He could imagine wandering through the trees with Ellery, teaching her about nature.

And it was his own damn fault that he hadn't had those experiences with her yet. He could have taken a more active role in her life, could have fought harder to get Rachel to let him spend more time with Ellery. Maybe this wouldn't have happened if he had. But he couldn't change the past. All he could do was go forward, but the idea of his and Ellery's future being subject to the whims of bureaucrats was tough to accept.

The worst part would be getting Rachel to relinquish custody. He hadn't even thought about her coming back and making more trouble. Hell, he didn't even know where she was. This all sucked. He downed half his can of Coke and set his snack aside. Closing his eyes, he tried to find some calm. His anger wasn't going to do Ellery or the situation any good. With his eyes shut, he became more in tune with the sounds around him. Birds chirping, the whisper of the breeze through the leaves… a dog yipping.

What dog? None of his neighbors owned a dog that he'd ever noticed. He opened his eyes and dropped his feet to the porch floor. And then he saw her. Imogen was a ways down the street, being half pulled, half dragged by an enormous puppy.

What the hell was she doing in his neighborhood? Aw, hell, for all he knew, she lived near him.

"Come on, Mr. Bubblesworth, you can't do that. Slow down." She was using a soothing tone that was having no effect on the dog. "Oh, please don't chew on your leash."

Sure enough, the dog had a firm grip on the leash. At the rate it was chomping away on the thin strip of leather, the restraint wouldn't last long. Patrick should have just gone into the house. This wasn't his problem, and he was in no mood to talk to anyone. Especially someone who had sat in that room earlier. She could have helped him out more with the other members of the panel, but she'd stayed mostly silent. Other than that one moment where she'd come to his defense.

"No, no, no," Imogen said as the dog picked up even more speed, jerking its head from side to side. Suddenly, the leash snapped.

Imogen dove to grab the dog, but it evaded her and bounded straight toward Patrick and his snack.

Oh, hell no, dog, Patrick thought. *I've had too much taken from me lately. You aren't getting my cheese.*

He stepped to the edge of the porch as the dog ran closer. Patrick kept his focus on the dog. In his peripheral vision, he could see Imogen running toward them, her hair flying loose, spare poop bags dangling from her pocket.

"Sit," he commanded when the dog had almost reached him. The authority in his voice had the dog's butt hitting the ground. Patrick reinforced the single word by stepping forward and laying his finger across the dog's nose to hold it in place.

"I'm so sorry," Imogen gasped. "Mr. Bubblesworth isn't very well trained yet."

"That's obvious," Patrick commented, keeping his eyes on the dog, who was panting from his antics. "Stay." He held out his hand to Imogen. "Give me the leash."

She handed it over. "It came with him from the pound. I haven't had a chance to get anything better." Her tone was apologetic.

The thin strap wasn't designed for a dog of this size. He folded it in half, shortening it but doubling its strength. Then he tied one end through a ring on the dog's collar with a Navy knot that nothing short of a hurricane could get loose. "This'll hold him for now," Patrick said, giving the leash back to Imogen. Now that the dog was taken care of, he looked fully at her for the first time. Her cheeks were pink from running, but it wasn't attraction he felt. Not this time. Instead, it was irritation.

"Thanks." Her phone buzzed in her pocket, and she jumped a bit, but she didn't take it out.

"Your dog is a beast," Patrick said, expecting a little more gratitude from her for his help in getting the animal under control.

"Don't be too hard on him." She dropped her hand to stroke the dog's ears. "He's only a puppy."

That was nice. She had all the sympathy in the world for a wayward mutt, but not for him and his daughter. He should let it go. Tell her to take her ridiculously named dog and leave. But that wasn't who he was. He wanted an answer from her.

"Why didn't you stick up for me more during that meeting?" he demanded.

She took a step back from him, looking offended. "I did what I could, but I had to tell the truth. I'm sure you can understand that."

"Understand that I'm not going to be a good father." He drilled her with a look.

"I never said that," she defended herself. "My desire first and foremost is for Ellery to be in the best situation possible."

"And that's not with me?"

"I didn't say that, either," she said. "I think you should get custody, and I said so. But your situation isn't without flaws. You're still in the military, right? What happens when you get deployed again? Ellery's already been abandoned once—if your childcare fell through and she had to go back into the foster system again, I don't know how she'd cope. That was so hard on her."

Guilt spiked through him for what Ellery had endured, but that wasn't going to happen again. He'd have a plan *and* a backup plan in place before his next deployment. He just needed to figure out what those were going to be.

Her phone buzzed a second time. This time, she took it out and jabbed a button, then shoved it back in her pocket before continuing. "Listen, I think the right decision was made today. I understand that it's not what you expected, but maybe you haven't thought through all the details yet. The benefits, I mean. Since CPS is going to stay involved, you'll have access to resources that you need."

"Resources? You mean people to tell me what to do." Having spent years in the military, he understood chain of command, but this wasn't a mission or a war. This was about his daughter.

"Yes, in the most positive sense. You'll be able to take a parenting course and learn about the needs of children Ellery's age." She hesitated for a second, as if expecting him to argue. He scowled but stayed silent, waiting for her to go on. "And you'll have access to counseling for Ellery. She has some behavioral issues. You saw that little tantrum in my classroom. Those are going to take time and professional help to work through."

"You said adjusting to school caused that in some kids." He flung her earlier words back in her face. "That it wasn't unusual."

"It isn't, necessarily, but Ellery's behaviors are more worrisome, especially after she ended up in foster care. She'll need counseling, and you can get that through CPS. They'll probably even require it."

"She'll be fine once she gets here with me," he said. Was he in over his head? Maybe a bit, he admitted to himself. But she was a little girl. How hard could this be?

"What's your plan to de-escalate a tantrum? Yell? Tell her to sit?" Imogen said with a pointed look at the dog. "You'll need a different approach with a traumatized child."

"Do you think that's what I would do?" he demanded. The control that he usually had no trouble maintaining was starting to slip. Her damn phone rang, and he forcibly stopped himself from shouting.

"Sorry, I meant to silence it," she said. "Wrong button." She tapped the screen again, hard, then turned toward him, her expression softening. "I think you don't know what to do. It's not intuitive."

"It seems easy enough for you," he said. Imogen made managing kids look simple. He'd been genuinely impressed with how she'd handled the glue incident.

"True," she said, smiling, "but I've been teaching for a while. I wasn't so good my first year—even though I'd gone to school and studied the theory. It takes practice. Trust me, if it hadn't been for some older and wiser teachers showing me the ropes, I would have failed utterly."

"So I'll ask for advice if I need it," he said. When hell froze over, he didn't add.

"Or you could recognize that you can't go it alone and get help from the beginning. You don't work alone as a SEAL, right? I don't know much about that world, but I thought you were in teams, with different people having different areas of specialization. CPS will give you the team you need in exchange for watching over you for a while. It's not a bad deal."

"Ellery needs the support, not me." He'd do what he needed to make Ellery's life better, but he didn't like asking for help for himself. He was impressed by her argument, though. She was smart to try to use an analogy that related to his life. Was that one of those things she'd learned by practicing?

"You both do," she said in a schoolteacher voice that didn't allow for argument.

They'd see about that, but he did feel a little better about the situation after hearing her perspective. Maybe today hadn't been as shitty as he'd originally thought.

Imogen tensed when her phone rang again.

"Aren't you going to answer?" he asked. "Seems like somebody really needs to reach you."

"No," she said, her shoulders rigid. "It's nothing I need to hear."

What was that about? "Let me see," he said, holding out his hand. Was an ex-boyfriend harassing her? She shook her head and huffed out a sigh. "Give me the phone," he repeated.

Her lips thinned into a line, but she handed it to him. He pressed the button to answer the call. Immediately, a masculine voice launched into a string of profanity-laced threats so harsh they made even Patrick blink, but he listened to every word until the line went dead. His gaze focused on Imogen. She had her head bent down, stroking the dog's ears, as if afraid to meet his eyes.

"Jesus, what was that?" he asked, stunned by the viciousness of what he'd heard.

"I…" She shuddered and didn't finish the sentence.

He looked at the call history, seeing a string of calls two or three minutes apart, from multiple numbers. This was a barrage, an attack. And the message he'd heard left his insides feeling cold. The caller had threatened—graphically—to maim or kill her if she didn't shut up and keep quiet. Shut up about what? What was a kindergarten teacher involved in that could generate that much hostility?

"They're just trying to scare me." Her voice was no more than a whisper.

"Is this connected to the note in your classroom?" He remembered her reaction to that. He'd thought it had been oddly intense, but clearly she had reason to be afraid.

"Yes," she admitted with a sigh. "Can you forget you ever heard that? Please."

"Not a chance." Protectiveness was wired into him. He couldn't ignore this. "Tell me what's going on," he demanded.

"I shouldn't," she said, looking around nervously, "but I've got no one I can trust."

He'd already scanned the area and seen nothing out of place, but their location was exposed. "Come inside," he said, knowing she'd be safer in his house, whatever the threat might be.

"Mr. Bubblesworth, too?" she asked with a glance at the oversized puppy.

"Him, too." Patrick went up the steps, opened the door, and waited for her and the dog to go through ahead of him. As soon as he locked the door behind them, he turned to her and waited for an explanation.

"I'm not supposed to talk about it," she said, fussing with the dog.

He took the leash, pulling the dog toward him, and waited. He had done enough interrogations to know that she was about to cave and tell him everything. All it took was a little patience and time, and she'd break.

"I…" She squeezed her eyes shut. "You can't tell anyone. Understand?" He nodded. "I'm supposed to testify at a trial this summer, but the person on trial is… powerful." She clutched one hand with the other. "And my testimony would be damaging for him. I don't know how he found out where I am, but he or his associates have been relentless."

"Are you in witness protection?" He took a guess, not quite believing it as he spoke, but it fit from what she'd said.

Her eyes sought his, and she didn't need to answer. It was written on her face.

"Have you reported the harassment to your handler?" he asked, knowing that an agent should be assigned to her, someone who could move her to a new place if necessary. They usually reacted quickly in such situations. "He should help you."

She gave a little snort. "I wouldn't count on it."

6

———————

Mr. Bubblesworth yanked on the leash in an attempt to get into Patrick's living room. "Sorry. I can take him," she said. "New environment, you know. Too much stimulation for a puppy."

"I'll manage him." Patrick glared down at the dog, and Mr. Bubblesworth whined softly and stilled. "Come in and sit." He led the way into the room and gestured for her to take a seat. He dropped into an armchair across from her, keeping the dog next to him.

She took a quick glance around the space. It was surprisingly homey in a worn, lived-in way. The furnishings were older, but in decent shape. She eyed them. With a little fabric and her sewing machine, she could recover the couch and chair, make some throw pillows, and elevate the surroundings to shabby chic. Maybe some swags on the windows.

What was she thinking? She wasn't his interior decorator. Still, sewing and creating were her refuge when times were tough. And they sure were that now. She'd been left with no support, which was the only explanation for her breaking the cardinal rule of witness protection and admitting that she was in it. Her handler had warned her against that, but then he'd done nothing to assist her since the constant threats began.

She shivered, remembering the note and the phone messages.

"What possessed you to get a dog while in witness protection?" Patrick's tone wasn't reassuring. "Is he part of your cover?"

"No." Didn't he understand her fear? He had to after listening to one of those calls. "I got him for protection. He's going to be huge and intimidating. A great guard dog."

Patrick looked at the dog doubtfully. "Yeah, right. In about five years, if you manage to train him."

"He's nice to have around," she said, losing some of her edge. "I've been… lonely, since it's impossible to make true friends when I'm living a lie." She was friendly with several of her fellow teachers, but she had to conceal too much about her background. Adding to that, most of them were several years older than she was. Her social life consisted of working at the food bank every other Saturday. No dates, no reason to wear her collection of beautiful shoes, no moment when she wasn't looking over her shoulder. She almost sighed.

"If the trial's this summer, you won't have to live like that for much longer," he pointed out.

"I could have waited it out, I guess," she admitted, "but when I saw a German shepherd puppy free on Craigslist, I couldn't resist. His picture was adorable."

"Imagine this home-wrecker of a dog being free." Patrick yanked the leash back just before Mr. Bubblesworth got his mouth around the remote control that sat on the arm of his chair.

Imogen felt a wave of irritation at the sarcastic comment. "Shepherds have strong bites, and I find that comforting. Remember, someone's out to get me." If they actually did half of what they threatened to, it was terrifying.

"Sorry," Patrick said. "Suppose you give me more details about your situation."

"I…" she hesitated, but she had to trust someone. "I left a school program one evening, and I planned to stop by Grant's office to surprise him."

"Grant?"

"My… ex-boyfriend," she said. "Anyway, I parked behind the construction company his father owned, and I was just about to get out of my car when I saw two guys drag a man toward an SUV. He was struggling, but weakly." She shivered. Her whole life had changed in that moment, and she hadn't even realized it. "When the car door opened, I glimpsed Grant's dad inside. The two thugs shoved the other guy in, and I saw then that his hands and feet were bound. It was like I was frozen. I didn't know what to do. Grant's dad had always treated me so well that I couldn't imagine that he was… hurting someone. So I went home and tried to rationalize it away. I almost called the police, but what would I have said?"

"And then what happened?" Patrick's voice was surprisingly gentle.

"Nothing, until two days later. I walked into the teachers' workroom and saw the local paper on the table. On the front, there was a picture of the man I'd seen, and the headline read that he was missing. I knew I couldn't be silent any longer. I left school and went straight to the police."

"Did they find the man?"

"Yeah. He'd been badly beaten, so badly that when he finally came out of the medically induced coma, he remembered almost nothing."

The weight of guilt hit her again "I wish… I wish I'd called the police that night, but I just didn't think that Grant's dad was a vicious man."

"So you can testify that you saw this man being held against his will by Grant's father?"

"Yes."

She'd thought about that day a million times, imagining how it could have turned out differently, constructing all sorts of "what if" scenarios. What if she hadn't stopped by that night? What if she'd parked in the front lot? What if she'd kept her mouth shut?

No, that she couldn't have done.

"All that was bad enough, but once the investigation began, I started getting threats, anonymous warnings not to testify. They were frightening enough that I told the district attorney's office about them. It turns out this case could be part of a bigger picture, something involving organized crime, so the government thought the risk warranted putting me in protection." She tried to smile, but it didn't work very well. "I'm not sure how much it's helped, but I guess it could be worse. After it's over," she continued, "I hope to get my life back. I was a teacher, just… elsewhere." She'd keep Mr. Bubblesworth, who'd settled down, dropping his nose to the rug with a groan. He'd be a reminder of this time, but not a sad one.

"Will you go home once it's over?" Patrick asked.

She shrugged. She couldn't think beyond the trial, and since there was no one special waiting for her there, she hadn't decided yet. Grant, perhaps understandably, had taken his father's side in the situation, so that was over.

"When did the threats start? I mean, the ones after you went into protection?"

The details seemed important to him, and talking about it—even though she knew she wasn't supposed to—was a relief, so she went on. "A couple months ago." She'd dismissed the first note as random, but then there had been more. "Some days there are only a few calls, and I think it might be over. And then I'll get a day like today. I think they're intensifying the campaign to scare me off."

"You've got to ask yourself if testifying is worth your life," he said. "That threat sounded real."

"I can't give up now. That would be wrong." Her moral code wouldn't allow it, and the district attorney had made clear that her testimony was essential to the case.

"And your handler's no help?"

She shook her head. "I asked—I told him when the threats started, and when they kept coming, but he said I just had to ignore them and wait it out."

"Which means relocation isn't an option," Patrick continued. "There must be someone you can trust. What about your family?"

"No one close. My parents are both gone." God, she missed them. They were quiet, strong people, and she'd wished time and again these past months that she could ask them for advice. But cancer had taken her mom three years ago, and her dad was hit by a car while jogging exactly one year after her mother's death. Since then, she'd felt cast adrift.

"I'm sorry," he said, sounding much more sympathetic than he'd been previously, and she realized she felt comfortable here in his living room. Not just comfortable, *safe* in a way she hadn't felt in... longer than she could remember. That sensation might come from him, though, not the place. She looked at him, and he must have seen something in her expression, because he left his chair and came to sit next to her. His arm went along the back of the couch, almost skimming her shoulders.

"I'm scared," she said, the words coming out easily with him so close. "I feel like there's no one left I can trust." His body heat and the scent of his spicy aftershave were reassurances, bits of comfort in a world that had had very little of that lately.

"You seem to trust me," he said, his voice quiet.

"I guess I do," she said, surprised at herself. She'd gotten out of the habit of trusting anyone, but he was different somehow.

"That'll make this easier," he said decisively and angled his body toward her. "I think you should come live here. If you're with me, I can protect you. Whoever is threatening you, I doubt they want to take me on."

"Live here?" Imogen echoed. "What—why would you suggest that?" She gave her head a shake, trying to make sense of his words. How did their conversation get here?

"It makes perfect sense. You need someone to get whoever's harassing you to back off, and I need help with Ellery... because you're right," he admitted. "I don't know much about raising little girls, and I could do with some guidance."

Oh. That made a certain amount of sense. Imogen knew and understood Ellery and her needs better than Patrick did. It might be a good exchange, even if it was sudden and... unusual. But moving in with a man she barely knew and adding childcare responsibilities to her work as a teacher was a big step. Not to mention... "What would CPS say to that?" she asked. "I think it would look odd to them." To say the least.

"Crap. You might be right." Patrick leaned against the back of the couch and dropped into silence. A muscle twitched in his jaw. What would he do if she reached out to soothe that—jump away? Come closer? She couldn't just leave them both sitting here awkwardly. Humor. Humor was always good to defuse tension. She'd learned that her first year teaching.

"Hey, we could get married," she joked. "CPS would love that. We'd look like a happy family, and your troubles would be over."

Imogen intended for him to laugh, but he snapped his fingers instead. "That's it. Talk about a win-win. We'll get married until the trial is over and you're safe. That'll give me time to arrange more permanent childcare. And by then, Ellery will be adjusted to living with me."

"Whoa, wait a minute here," Imogen said, trying to put the brakes on this runaway train. "You can't be serious."

"You bet I am." His dark eyes were on her, drawing her in, but she had to resist, because this was ridiculous. "It would last maybe a year. That would guarantee your troubles would be over. I have six months before I go out on a mission again, and then you can be here during my deployment to make it all go smoothly for Ellery. When I get back, we'll get a divorce."

"You make this sound simple, but it's not." She didn't have experience with marriage and divorce, but she was sure it was much more complicated than he was suggesting, especially with a child involved.

"Do you have a better solution?" he asked. "One that addresses both our problems so well?"

She didn't, of course, so she pointed out the obvious. "No, but we're not responsible for each other, either. I don't owe you anything, and vice versa."

He shook his head. "Now that I know what kind of trouble you're in, I can't turn my back on you."

Great, just what she needed: a man who was hardwired to help. Imogen was willing to admit that she wasn't managing very well on her own with the threats, but that didn't mean this hare-brained scheme was the answer. "Give me a minute to think."

She got up and paced toward the windows that looked out onto the front porch. The pretty lace curtains were old, but clean. Idly, she stroked the fabric, her fingers running over the texture as her mind processed his offer. She tried to list all the reasons she should reject his suggestion and weigh them against the benefits. The scales tipped in one direction.

"Is it your boyfriend?" Patrick asked quietly from behind her.

"Ex-boyfriend," she said. "Grant thought I should have kept my mouth shut about what I saw. I guess I can understand… not wanting to think your own father was doing something wrong." Still, she and Grant had been dating for a year. It hadn't been a passionate relation-ship, but it had been solid, or so she'd thought. It had been a disap-pointment when she realized Grant had never even considered standing by her.

She swallowed, pushing away her memories of being used by others because she was nice. Her experiences with that had started when she was ten, and the adult world hadn't changed her thinking. Most people only engaged with others for their own benefit. At least in this situation, she and Patrick would both gain something.

Despite her misgivings, she had to admit that Patrick's plan made a certain amount of sense, in practical terms. But it was a big step. Marriage. To an attractive guy.

Not a real marriage. It would be in name only.

She turned from the window and studied him. He hadn't moved, but he looked ready to spring into action if it were needed. She really couldn't ask for a better barrier between her and those incessant, awful threats. Okay, maybe she could do this.

"I come with an oversized, mostly untrained puppy," she said.

"I can live with that, but I'm not calling him Mr. Bubblesworth." The dog lifted its head at his name. "Stay, Mr. B," Patrick commanded before rising and walking to Imogen. He rested his hands on her shoulders, a move that was surprisingly intimate. "Was that a yes?"

"Yes," she said. "I will marry you, but in name only, and only until the court case is done and Ellery is settled." Clear boundaries were essential if this was going to work.

7

———————

"But what about Goldie?" Ellery wailed, standing in the middle of Patrick's living room. "I want Goldie."

"You've got to give me some details here," he said to his daughter. He'd picked her up from the foster home earlier, and she'd been all smiles until they arrived home. He'd hauled what little she owned into the house. Two duffel bags, a plastic tub of toys, an art portfolio, and a stuffed orange dog that she was clutching so hard that Patrick felt sorry for the toy. "Is your dog named Goldie?"

"No," Ellery's pitch went up, which he wouldn't have thought possible. "He's Oscar. Goldie's a fish."

Patrick had seen a goldfish bowl on the kitchen counter at the foster home. "Are you talking about Mrs. Ryan's fish? The one in the kitchen?"

"Yes," she shrieked, and he held up his hands in the universal symbol to calm down. Apparently, that was a language Ellery didn't speak, because her screams got louder.

"The fish isn't ours, and I don't do fish. Besides, he's better off with Mrs. Ryan." Although Patrick was nearly shouting to make himself heard over Ellery's cries, what he said seemed perfectly reasonable to him. It had no effect on Ellery, who threw herself on the floor, almost hitting her head on the brick hearth, and started to roll around and scream about the fish and how unfair he was being.

So this was a temper tantrum, Patrick thought, trying to be objective. Great, he'd identified the problem, but he had no idea how to fix it. He got closer so she was at his feet. All his instincts said to pick her up and restrain her, but she was squirming and rolling so much he didn't see how he could do that without hurting her.

"Stop that," he shouted. "You're being ridiculous. It's just a fish," he commanded, in a voice that could make hardened SEALs jump. No effect. Ellery screamed, and tears flowed from her eyes. Her foot connected hard with his calf, making him wince. Dammit.

"Need some help?" Imogen's voice cut through the turmoil, and he turned to see her standing in the doorway with Mr. B on a leash.

"God, yes," he said, grateful for someone sensible.

"Stand back." Imogen unclipped the dog, letting him bound into the room. Seconds later the oversized puppy was licking Ellery's face, and the girl's crying and yelling turned to laughter.

"What the heck?" He watched the scene before him in amazement, then walked closer to Imogen. Her dark blonde hair was pulled up in a ponytail, and she looked young. She'd be his bride soon, and that thought hit him like a ton of bricks. He'd kept busy for the past few days, getting Ellery's and Imogen's bedrooms ready. As he worked, he'd pondered the proposition he'd made. It seemed like a good deal for both of them, but what would it be like to live with a pretty woman, one he was attracted to, without any kind of sexual or romantic relationship? He had no experience with that sort of thing.

"Distraction. It works almost every time," she said. "Give her a few minutes, and then you should be able to talk with her about why she got so upset."

"I think it was because she wanted the foster mom's goldfish."

"Ah, Goldie." Imogen gave a little nod of understanding. "Ellery drew pictures of the fish in class. Animals are often a source of comfort for kids in tough situations. It's why I let my class name Mr. Bubblesworth."

"You took that beast to school?" He imagined the amount of destruction the dog could cause in her tidy classroom.

"No." She smiled, seeming to know what he was picturing. "I showed photos and video of him. I would like to train him as a therapy dog, though. Some schools are using those very effectively to help kids."

"It helped here," he said, with a glance at Ellery. She was sitting on the floor, her back against the couch, with Mr. B sprawled across her lap.

"Time for that talk," Imogen said and moved forward so Ellery could see her. She plopped onto the floor next to the little girl. Patrick followed and sat across from them.

"Mr. Bubblesworth is happy to see me," Ellery said. Her cheeks were streaked with dried tears, and her hair was a mess.

"Of course he is." Imogen gave Mr. B's ears a rub. "He likes you, and so do I, which is why it makes me sad to see you behave like that. What were you upset about?"

Ellery's lower lip began to tremble, and Patrick prepared himself for another tantrum.

"Remember to use your words." Imogen's voice was gentle.

"Goldie's not here," Ellery whispered.

"I know," Imogen said, expressing sympathy with her tone and look, "and that's too bad, but she wasn't your fish to bring here. Remember when we talked about the things that were ours and the things that weren't, at school?"

Ellery nodded. "I just liked her."

"I'm sure you did. Maybe later today you could draw a picture of Goldie to remind yourself of her and hang it on the refrigerator," Imogen suggested.

The only things on Patrick's fridge were takeout menus, but if a fish picture made Ellery happy, he'd stick five of them up there. He wasn't up for another tantrum. Ever. He doubted he'd be that lucky, and he was glad to have Imogen here, since he had no idea how to defuse that kind of bomb.

"Okay," Ellery wiped away fresh tears with the back of her hand.

"Why don't you go to the bathroom and wash your face now?" Imogen suggested. "We have a lot of work to do to get moved in today."

Without another word, Ellery got up and headed for the downstairs bathroom. As soon as the water was running, Patrick leaned closer to Imogen, who now had the dog on her lap, and whispered, "You have to teach me how to do that."

"You'll get the hang of it." She smiled at him. "Be patient. She's had a rough couple months, and I don't know what her life was like before she went into foster care. Not good, I suspect."

Patrick had a better sense of that and could guess Rachel had made their daughter feel unwelcome, a burden, in the time before she ran off with her dream man. The bitter anger he felt toward both Rachel and himself over that wouldn't do Ellery any good. His goal now was to learn how to be a dad. He'd have to watch how Imogen handled the girl and try to mimic it. He knew he was out of his element. He would think nothing of taking down an armed assailant—he was trained to do that—but dealing with an emotionally fragile six-year-old scared the hell out of him.

When Ellery returned from the bathroom, Imogen stood up. "Let's get moved in, Ellery. I've got boxes and such in my car, but let's get your stuff upstairs first. Have you seen your bedroom yet?"

Patrick was ashamed to admit they hadn't gotten past the down-stairs. He led the way up. The master bedroom was on the right side, along with a bathroom, and the left side had two smaller bedrooms.

"Ellery, this is your room." He went to the smaller one that faced out the front. Cautiously, she peeped in. "Do you remember being here?" It had been almost two years ago since she'd been allowed to spend the night at his house.

"The purple room." Her smile was huge when she went in. This had been the fancy guest room in his grandmother's day, with lavender wallpaper and bedding, and a wooden floor painted white. Ellery climbed onto the bed, and Mr. B jumped up with her. He didn't like the idea of letting the dog on the furniture, but the idea of another tantrum if he objected made him hold his tongue. He could fight that battle when his ears weren't still ringing from the last one.

"Am I next door?" Imogen asked.

"Across the hall," he said as they stepped out of Ellery's room.

"Isn't this the master?" she asked, taking in the queen bed and more-modern furniture.

"I thought you'd want some space for yourself." The night before, he'd moved his things into the other small room to give Imogen more privacy.

"Thanks, that was really thoughtful of you." She put her purse on the dresser. "But where does that leave you?"

"In what was my room when I visited as a kid. This was my grand-mother's house." His old room only had a twin bed, but that didn't bother him. He could sleep just about anywhere, and the room had the comfort of familiarity, with its blue walls and dark furnishings.

"Ah," she said, a sudden smile showing. "That makes sense. It didn't have the feel of a single man's home."

"I'll start hauling up things from your car," he said, not surprised that she was observant.

"Get Ellery's stuff first, and I'll help her settle in."

With a nod, he went downstairs and began the process of moving them in. He watched as Imogen guided Ellery's behavior from every-thing about where to put her toy bin to what afternoon snack to have. In the kitchen, he'd seen Ellery start to lurch out of control again, but Imogen deftly brought her back by giving her two healthy choices and letting her pick.

Once again, he thanked his lucky stars. The whole situation was chaotic, but it seemed as if it could work—with Imogen's help. And, as a bonus, he hadn't missed the occasional glances she gave him when she thought he wasn't looking. There was something nice about getting the attention of a pretty woman, and he couldn't deny his attraction to her.

By seven, everyone was settled, and the house felt full, but orderly. His grandmother would have loved it.

"Time to eat," he called when the pizza delivery guy dropped off two boxes. By the time they came downstairs, he had pizza on plates, beer for the adults, and a glass of milk for Ellery. It wasn't the greatest family meal, but it was a start. That was, after he exiled Mr. B to the backyard. He didn't need a drooling puppy circling the table and begging for food.

"I'm wiped," Imogen said. "Moving's hard." She brushed Ellery's hair back from her face so it wouldn't be in her pizza.

"One job done. Monday's job is getting married." Two pairs of female eyes met his. He read shock in both of them. What had he said? School had let out for summer the previous week, so Imogen didn't have to work. What was wrong with a Monday wedding?

"You can't just get married like that," Ellery insisted with a dramatic eye roll.

"We're only going to the courthouse," he said, wondering what the big deal was. "I looked it up earlier." He tapped his phone open and found the page he'd skimmed about civil weddings. He read it more carefully this time and saw that appointments were required. "We do need an appointment. I didn't see that before. Nothing's available until Tuesday at four. Will that do?" He eyed his daughter.

"I can work with that," Ellery declared, as if she planned weddings every day. He almost laughed at her, but he caught Imogen's warning glance. Ellery focused on Imogen, her face serious. "What kind of silhouette do you want?"

"Huh?" What language were they talking now?

"I hadn't thought about that," Imogen responded, ignoring his confusion. "Something simple, I think. I'm not the ball gown type, and I'm not a fan of the mermaid look."

"Sequins?" Ellery bounced up in her chair as she talked. "Lace? It wouldn't be much of a wedding without those. Can I be your bridesmaid?" Her face flattened with disappointment. "But I only have one dress, and it's ugly."

"I'm sure we can fix that," Imogen said. "We won't have Randy and the designers, but I'm pretty handy with a sewing machine."

"Who's Randy?" Patrick interrupted to ask, a little nervous about the excitement on Imogen's face.

"*Say Yes to the Dress*." Ellery shot him a superior look. "It's a show."

"In the morning, we'll make a list of what we need, and then we'll do a little shopping," Imogen said to Ellery. "Go put on your pajamas and brush your teeth. Better make it an early night, because we've got a lot to do tomorrow."

Ellery shot off, leaving the adults at the table.

"*Say Yes to the Dress*?" he questioned, assuming that Imogen had to be pacifying his daughter with her part in the discussion.

"It's a reality show filmed at a bridal salon," Imogen explained. "Women come to try on dresses and find the perfect one. It's super popular."

"Sounds awful," he declared.

"You're not exactly the target audience." Imogen rose from her seat and gathered their plates, and he wondered if he'd made a mistake or misjudged her. Was she the romantic type? He hoped not.

"Do you want that?" he asked, worried. "My plan is to keep this uncomplicated. We'll just go, get married, and get back to our lives." He heard her sigh as she opened the dishwasher to load it. He wasn't great at reading women, but he could guess her sigh meant that she did want it. He had to hit this head-on. "Talk to me."

"Every wedding should have some fanfare," she said, coming back to the table and taking her seat again, "even if it's a fake wedding. It doesn't have to be excessive or expensive, but dresses and flowers are kind of a must."

He nodded, accepting the inevitable, but inside he wondered if he was going to regret floating the idea of marriage, much less following through on it. That thought competed in his head with the idea that she'd be a beautiful bride.

8

———————

"Imogen Mendel and Patrick Nelson," Imogen said to the woman in the office on the third floor of the county courthouse on Tuesday afternoon. "Has my fiancé checked in yet? I don't see him."

"Not yet," the woman responded with a smile. "Don't worry, he'll be here. I've been working this job for twenty years. Brides are jittery and the ones likely to run for it, not grooms. They come through in the end."

Imogen smoothed the white satin of the gown she wore. Jittery was a good way of describing how she felt, since she had to be the first woman in the history of weddings who was getting married to protect herself against a corrupt witness protection system. Well, that was half the reason. She smiled at Ellery, the other, better reason. Being married to Patrick would help him keep his daughter and become a better father.

"You look like a princess," the woman said to Ellery, who wore a dress of Cinderella blue, including a tulle skirt. "Are you the flower girl?"

"Bridesmaid," Ellery said, giving the woman a dramatic curtsy.

"Of course. Congratulations," the woman offered.

"Let's wait over there." Imogen pointed to an area nearby, where a shaft of sunlight came in through a high window. When they reached it, Ellery began fussing with Imogen's gown. No doubt she'd seen that on the show, but Imogen didn't mind. With only a day to pull off their looks, she thought she'd done well. Her dress, which she'd purchased at a resale shop, had needed very little alteration. It was a white sheath that fell from spaghetti straps and skimmed over her body to the floor. She'd dug out a pair of high-heeled silver sandals to go with it and felt quite bridal.

Ellery's outfit had taken more effort. They had found a discarded prom dress in a thrift store. Imogen had cut the sequined bodice off and used the skirt material to fashion an entirely new dress for the little girl. In a burst of creativity the evening before, they'd taken apart the bodice and formed it into bases for the bouquets they carried. Some white tissue paper flowers finished the job.

"Your idea for the bouquets was outstanding," Imogen told Ellery. The girl had an eye for color and design, and Imogen had been glad to use her skills to create such beauty. After all, this was her first wedding, and she wanted it to be special and happy, even if it wasn't quite real. "Do you think your dad will wear the outfit we put out for him?" They'd left dress pants and a button-down shirt hanging on the back of his door.

Ellery gave a sage nod. "Of course he will."

Imogen wasn't as confident, since he'd avoided them during their day of shopping and sewing. He'd left the house a few hours earlier, claiming he had errands to run, and he'd meet them at the courthouse. She wished he'd get here, since she was anxious to get this partnership started. One year of marriage. They'd both gain from it, and she promised herself to do her best to make it as pleasant as possible.

A gasp next to her drew Imogen's eyes down to Ellery. The girl was staring toward the entrance from the hallway. Imogen let her eyes follow Ellery's and felt her heart almost stop. Patrick wasn't wearing the nice outfit they'd left for him. He was in his full Navy dress uniform. The jacket had gold trim on the cuffs and medals—so many medals—pinned to the chest. She'd known he was a SEAL, but he must have been a highly decorated one. His bling put her bouquet to shame, but it also reminded her that this man could and would protect her.

All talk in the room ceased as every eye went to him. As if he didn't notice, he strode toward her and Ellery, a man confident and so damned attractive she thought she might melt from the heat.

"Nelson and Mendel?" a voice called from the far end of the room.

"That's us," he said. When he reached her, he offered his arm in a formal gesture.

Patrick could barely breathe. Where had Imogen managed to find a wedding dress that fit her like a glove, overnight? He'd seen her in teacher clothes at school and yoga pants at the house and was completely unprepared for Imogen dressed up in a gown that revealed a body he was pretty sure he'd kill for.

Ellery fell in step on his other side and gave him a knowing smile. The little minx. She'd known what she was up to by insisting on wedding clothing and a fuss.

"You look very pretty," he said to his daughter, and her smile ramped up to one of pure pleasure at the compliment.

"So do you," she replied.

He didn't know about pretty for him, but he was glad that he'd made the decision to wear his uniform. When he'd stopped at home to change, he'd seen the pants and shirt they expected him to wear, but he thought the occasion deserved better. Despite his resistance the other night, he'd realized that his wedding, likely the only one he'd ever have, should be taken seriously and celebrated. He owed that to Imogen, considering the effort she was making to help him with Ellery.

"And you're beautiful," he whispered to Imogen as they walked. A soft pink blush rose on her skin, making her even more lovely.

"Oh," she exclaimed softly when they entered the room where the ceremony would be held. The courthouse building was old, and this chamber showed that, with its intricately laid marble floor and a large ornate fireplace at one end. Rich dark wood paneled the walls. It was far nicer than he expected, which made him glad for her and himself.

Ellery swirled around in front of him, stopping their progress. "You have to go up there, so that me and Imogen can walk down the aisle."

"It's not that kind…" he started, but when Ellery crossed her arms in front of her, he gave up. "Yes, ma'am." He walked to the judge and shook hands with him before turning back to the two women in his life.

Ellery took her place in front of Imogen and walked slowly toward him. He was impressed with what a little lady she was, not the wild child he'd dealt with in the past few days. She reached him and waved to Imogen to come. With a smile fitting a bride, Imogen held her bouquet and moved gracefully to him. As soon as she was in front of the judge, she slipped her hand in his and gave it a squeeze.

"Imogen Mendel and Patrick Nelson," the judge said, "today you enter this room as individuals, but you will leave here as husband and wife, blending your lives, expanding your family ties, and embarking upon the grandest adventure of human interaction. The story of your life together is still yours to write."

As much as Patrick knew their union wasn't the one described, he wanted to take the words to heart.

"Remember to treat yourselves and each other with respect," the judge continued, "and remind yourselves often of what brought you together. Take responsibility for making the other feel safe, and give the highest priority to the tenderness, gentleness, and kindness that your connection deserves."

Imogen's fingers tightened around his when the word "safe" was used, a reminder of why she was here… but was there anything else to it? In that moment, he felt there was.

"You may repeat after me." The judge turned to him. "I, Patrick, take Imogen to be my wife, my partner in life and my one true love." He paused after each sentence, waiting for Patrick to echo his words. "I will trust you and respect you, laugh with you and cry with you, loving you faithfully through good times and bad, regardless of the obstacles we may face together. I give you my hand, my heart, and my love, from this day forward, for as long as we both shall live."

Patrick spoke the lines clearly, even if love might not play into what they had. Overcoming obstacles and giving her his trust and respect were things he could promise her. Her gaze was steady on his as she spoke her vows in turn, and he'd have given anything to know what she was thinking.

"It is now time for the rings," the judge said.

Imogen handed Ellery her bouquet while Patrick pulled the rings from his jacket pocket. At the jewelry store, he'd thought the simple gold bands were good enough for a temporary marriage. Now, he wished he'd made a better choice for her, something more special to match her beauty and express his gratitude.

He slipped the ring on her finger and repeated the words spoken by the judge: "I give you this ring as a symbol of my love and faithfulness. As I place it on your finger, I commit my heart and soul to you."

A moment later, she placed a matching ring on his finger and the judge spoke the final words. "By the authority vested in me by the State of South Carolina, I pronounce you husband and wife. You may now kiss the bride."

The kiss. Somehow he'd forgotten about that part, not that he minded the opportunity to kiss her. She raised an eyebrow at him a fraction of an inch, and her lips curved up at the corners.

"Kiss her, Daddy," Ellery said. "You have to. It's the rule."

Patrick touched the smooth skin of her cheek with his fingertips as their lips came together. Hers were soft and inviting, making him want more. The kiss started off tentative, but the spark of attraction between them quickly turned into the fire of desire. Despite that, he kept the contact brief. Later, maybe his bride would let him have another kiss, one that wasn't witnessed by his daughter and the judge.

9

Imogen slowly backed away from their kiss. She opened her eyes and met his. Was that desire in their dark depths? If so, it matched what she was feeling. Their wedding ceremony had far exceeded her expectations. She wondered for a moment if the marriage would as well, then shook off the thought. No way of telling, and she couldn't go into this assuming it meant more than they'd agreed.

"We need pictures," Ellery announced.

"I'd be happy to take some," the judge volunteered. Patrick handed over his phone and they posed for pictures, some with Ellery and some without. After signing the paperwork, they thanked the judge and walked out of the courthouse.

"Now what?" Ellery asked as they stood on the sidewalk.

"I'm willing to bet you have a plan," Patrick said.

"We should have a nice dinner," she declared. "I think the Hartsville Café is the perfect place."

"Have you been there?" Imogen asked, somewhat surprised Ellery would suggest the trendy little bistro located in the downtown area, just a short walk away.

"Daddy took me there for my birthday." Ellery's voice got quieter. "It was really pretty."

"I'm surprised you remember that," Patrick said, looking pleased.

"It's a lovely place," Imogen said. "Okay with you, Patrick?"

"Of course. Do you want to walk?" His eyes swept down her body, ending at her toes peeking out from under her gown. "Your shoes aren't…"

She laughed, although she appreciated his concern. "I could run in these. Don't worry about me. Since it's a nice day, let's walk." She took one of Patrick's hands, and Ellery took the other.

As they went through town, people in passing cars beeped their horns, waved, and called, "Congratulations!"

"I like living in a smaller place," Imogen said. She'd grown up in a city more than twice the size of Hartsville, and she enjoyed the sense of community here.

"I miss it when I'm away," Patrick said as he waved to a well-wisher. "But I gotta say that I feel like a spectacle at the moment."

She laughed. "I think that's acceptable every once in a while."

"Here we are," Ellery announced when they reached the café. The façade was painted a deep green, and flower boxes showed off masses of blooms beneath the large front windows.

Inside, the waitstaff greeted them warmly and seated them in a quiet corner, paying what Imogen imagined was extra attention to every detail. Candles and flowers arrived at their table, and the café manager even surprised them with beautifully plated slices of cake for dessert.

Throughout the meal, Ellery kept up a steady stream of chatter about the wedding, her dress, Mr. Bubblesworth, and anything else that came to her mind. Imogen was used to this from her experience as a teacher, but she was mildly surprised at the way Patrick kept smiling and encouraging his daughter to talk. He was doing better at this dad thing already.

With many thanks, they left the café and drove their respective cars home. "She's out," Patrick said when they met up in the driveway.

Ellery's eyelids fluttered open. "I'm sleepy," the girl murmured and held out her arms for her father to carry her. It was still light outside, but the little girl was done for the day. Too much excitement.

Patrick carried her into the house and up the stairs, Imogen following them.

"I'll help her get her dress off," Imogen said.

"Night night, Daddy," Ellery said as Patrick kissed her cheek.

"I didn't spill on my fancy dress," Ellery said proudly as she climbed into bed a few minutes later.

"You were a perfect little lady today. I'm proud of you." Imogen pulled the sheet up to tuck it around Ellery.

"I'm glad you're my new mommy," the girl murmured sleepily.

Imogen swallowed hard. She'd thought of herself as Patrick's wife and Ellery's caregiver, but not as her mother. She felt a pang of guilt, because it would be hard on Ellery when the marriage ended. For now, though, she'd give the girl what she could and help Patrick form a bond with his daughter.

"Goodnight, sweetie," she whispered and left the room.

In the upstairs hallway, she paused. Should she change out of her gown? She didn't want to. The dress was beautiful, and it felt so good against her skin. Why not keep it on for the rest of the evening? She headed downstairs and stopped when she reached the living room. A bottle of champagne and two glasses sat on the coffee table. Nice, if unexpected. Patrick stood by the fireplace, watching her.

"Hi," she said, feeling both shy and surprised. He'd been surprising her all day—from when he showed up in his uniform, to the kiss, to his convivial attitude about Ellery and her plans. Their marriage was a means to an end, but he seemed to be willing to play along. And that warmed her heart. "I didn't expect this."

He gave a little shrug. "I came to my senses sometime late yesterday and decided that you and Ellery were right. Weddings should be celebrated. Champagne?"

"I've love some," she said and took a seat on the couch. He poured the wine and sat next to her.

"What should our toast be?" he asked as he handed her a glass.

"*To us* is the obvious choice for wedding days, but ours might be a bit more complicated."

"How about *to us forming a successful partnership,* then?" he suggested.

"That'll work." She tapped her glass to his and took a sip. The champagne was good. She took another drink and leaned back against the cushion, relaxing for the first time in hours. In the days since she'd moved in, they had very little downtime. Ellery was around, or they were both busy with other things. This was different. Pleasant, good… maybe something a little more than that. She studied Patrick's handsome face. He'd shed the jacket to his uniform, but he still wore the dress shirt and trousers. She wanted another kiss from him, she couldn't deny that. What would he do if she leaned in?

She shouldn't. He'd kissed her at the courthouse because it was an expectation at weddings. It hadn't meant anything, not really. She had seen his appreciation for the way she looked, though.

"Ellery's choice of restaurants was good. What birthday did you take her there?" she asked, to keep her mind off other thoughts.

"Her fifth. I had a short leave, enough to be here for her birthday and Halloween before I shipped out again. I didn't realize young kids remembered details like that."

"They remember plenty," she said. "Especially ones as mentally quick as Ellery. She's bright. Your challenge will be guiding her intelligence in the right direction."

"Your challenge, too, for the next year. Have I mentioned how grateful I am?" His face became serious. "By the way... we should have talked about this before. I know this isn't a real marriage, but I think we should be exclusive while it lasts."

"Makes sense," she said, pondering his meaning of exclusive. It was different from the norm, because they weren't really a couple. "CPS wouldn't like it if they caught wind of one of us breaking our marriage vows. Not dating is no hardship for me."

"You've got to have guys lined up." His eyes swept over her.

She took another sip of champagne, flattered at the compliment, but it wasn't the case. Grant had been her first serious relationship. "Not in my current circumstances. Grant and I were talking about marriage, but obviously that ended."

"Was he awful about it?" he asked.

She nodded, recalling the bitter scene. Grant had pleaded with her, saying he loved her and begging her not to testify. When she refused to change her mind, his demeanor had changed and he'd made some brutal comments about her. Maybe he was more like his dad than she'd recognized while they were together.

"I'm sorry for that." Patrick looked more angry than sorry.

"I guess it was understandable, in a way," she said.

"Would you have married him?"

"I don't know. I was lonely when I started dating him. Hurting. My parents had both died in a short time. I wanted someone of my own, I guess, and he seemed like it." She'd met Grant a month after her father's funeral, and he'd seemed like a knight in shining armor. He hadn't been, and she was relieved to have discovered that before they became more involved. "What about you and Ellery's mom?"

His face clouded for a minute, and she wasn't sure he'd answer.

"Rachel and I had an on-again," he started, "off-again thing that was never serious. When I was on leave, we'd go out. She liked to party and was a lot of fun. It's hard to remember that now. Anyway, I came home from a short mission, and she announced she was pregnant with my baby. I was floored. I never expected that. And what's more, she didn't want to keep the baby."

Imogen couldn't contain her gasp. What if Ellery had never been born? The world would be a bit dimmer. "I'm glad you convinced her to change her mind."

"Me too. It took some sweet-talking. I promised to support them financially and do whatever I could when I was home, but it all went sideways from the beginning. Rachel made demands, a lot of them unreasonable, and we fought whenever we were in the same room. We decided when Ellery was three that it was better if we saw her separately, which worked for a while, but as time went on, Rachel seemed to get more and more frustrated—with me, with Ellery, I don't know. It didn't make any sense. You'd think she'd have wanted me to spend more time with Ellery, not less—so she could have time to herself—but instead she started trying to totally shut me out of Ellery's life."

"That must have been hard." Imogen couldn't imagine how awful that must have been.

"In some ways I felt I deserved it. I'd been an absentee father. I mean, I cared about Ellery, but I'd never made any serious effort to make her a bigger part of my life. But when Rachel tried to cut me off, I decided I needed to make some changes for both our sakes, Ellery's and mine. When I came back from my most recent deployment, I intended to fight Rachel for joint custody."

"And you found a mess instead," she concluded. "Were you surprised Rachel had run off?"

"Not really. I wish I could say I was. But she was always looking for something better, and she never liked being a mom. She made that painfully clear to me and probably to Ellery, too. I have a lot to make up for with my little girl."

"Children can be very forgiving." She reached for his hand, covering it with hers.

"I hope you're right about that," he said. "Sometimes when she gets temperamental, I can see Rachel's worst qualities in her."

"Did you consider marrying Rachel when she got pregnant?" Imogen had seen some marriages that started like that and ended up working out.

"No. As you can guess, Rachel wasn't the marrying kind—and being married to a SEAL is tough. My teammates who are married have strong, committed relationships. I knew Rachel and I were never going to have that."

"It must be tough to keep a relationship going when one of the people is away for months at a time. I can't imagine that."

"It's going to happen to us before we're done," he said, turning his hand over to clasp hers.

"But that's not the same," she said. "We know this is a practical arrangement. We're not trying to maintain love, which apparently neither of us has had much success with."

"You're right about that. We're probably making the smarter choice by marrying for responsible reasons rather than being swept away by passion."

She considered that a moment, trying to figure out how it was that she could simultaneously agree and disagree with his statement. "Passion is a serious word, but attraction would be okay, wouldn't it?" she finally asked. She hadn't imagined that tug between them. She was sure of it.

He gave her a slow grin. "Oh, no argument there. I definitely felt attracted when I first saw you in that dress. And during our kiss." He placed their glasses on the table and leaned closer to her. "I'd like to try that again."

He held still a moment, seeming to search her eyes for permission, and then his mouth closed over hers. He tasted of man and champagne, a heady combination that made her lean into him and grip his shoulders. His response was immediate, hands cradling her head as he deepened the kiss. His tongue slid into her mouth, hot and inviting. She had no idea how long they kissed; all she had was a sensation that, she feared, could easily go beyond attraction. Did it reach passion? She wasn't sure. Passion was a dangerous game, one she didn't think she was ready for.

"I think I'd better say good night," she whispered when the kiss ended.

He stood and tugged her to her feet. "That's probably wise. Good night, Imogen." He kissed her again briefly before breaking the contact between them.

10

———————

When Imogen woke the next morning, she rolled over in the big bed and eyed her wedding dress where she'd left it hanging from a hook to air. She'd really gotten married the day before, making her, Patrick, and Ellery a family of sorts. Ellery's reference to her being a mother came back to her, and she sighed, trying to think how best to navigate that issue in a way that would be helpful for Ellery. She guessed she was a stepmother, though only a temporary one. The next few days would be crucial in sorting out her role in the household to both father and daughter.

She thought about the kiss she and Patrick had shared. She'd take *that* role anytime. And then there was their conversation before the kiss, where she'd seen a more emotionally available side of Patrick. He'd been open, revealing his past, and so had she. It had felt good, after a year of keeping to herself, to confide in someone. Nothing during her time in witness protection had felt like it was truly hers. She often felt she was living someone else's life.

Was she doing that with this marriage as well? Probably. She took a deep breath and forced herself out of bed. Today was the day for her to establish her place in this household.

After a quick shower, she headed for the kitchen. Before she reached it, the scent of coffee and the sound of bickering reached her. Being the peacemaker seemed like her first job.

"This stuff is gross," Ellery said, shoving at the cereal in her bowl with her spoon. "I'm not eating it."

"Try it. It's good for you." Patrick's voice suggested his patience was wearing thin.

"Good morning." Imogen pulled out her super happy kindergarten teacher voice and got two different reactions. Patrick's expression said, "Thank God, another adult," and Ellery's was stubborn belligerence that said, "Nothing is going to pacify me."

"Good morning," Patrick said. "Ellery's not happy with her breakfast."

"I can see that." Great, she was going to have to play referee before coffee. Alas. "Ellery, did you ask politely for a different cereal?"

"No," the girl snapped, and the tension in the room rose.

"I think that would be a good place to start," Imogen suggested before Patrick could react. "Do you remember the expression I used in school? You catch more flies with honey than you do with vinegar. I think you really liked the bulletin board we made where the flies and bees and butterflies all flocked to the honey, but they all stayed away from the nasty-tasting vinegar."

"Yeah," Ellery admitted.

"What was the point?" Imogen had created the bulletin board to teach the kids a lesson about appropriate behavior. Her students had fun cutting out the insects and coloring them. Ellery's had been an extrav-agant butterfly in orange and purple.

"Being nice and sweet gets you what you want," Ellery mumbled.

"Not all the time," Imogen said with a smile at the girl's interpreta-tion, "but it's a good start. Try again."

"Daddy," Ellery said in a sweet-as-pie voice, "may I please have a different cereal?"

"That's the only kind I have. Sorry, kiddo," he said. Imogen heard him mutter that there had been a discount at Costco.

"Being sweet didn't do me any good," Ellery complained to Imogen.

"Didn't it?" Imogen was opening cabinets and assessing items in the pantry. "You see, now that you've been nice, I could be persuaded to make pancakes. What do you think of that?"

"Yes, please!" Ellery hopped out of her chair, dashed to Imogen, and wrapped her arms around her waist.

"That okay with you?" Imogen asked Patrick.

"Fine," he said. "I'll just plan on running an extra mile later to burn off the fat."

"Uh-huh." Imogen gave him a thorough up-and-down look that he couldn't have missed the meaning of. The man didn't have an ounce of fat on him. He was lean and ripped. At least, it sure looked that way, and the fitted T-shirt and jeans he wore gave her a pretty clear view.

"Can I help?" Ellery tilted her face up.

"Of course. No one cooks alone. Get milk and eggs from the refrigerator." When the girl moved away, Imogen grabbed a bowl and began assembling the batter. Making pancakes with a six-year-old took longer than it would have if Imogen had worked alone, but Ellery's mood adjusted in the time it took to put a platter of perfectly round pancakes on the table.

As they dug into breakfast, Ellery chatted about her plans for the day, which seemed to center around playing with Mr. Bubblesworth in the backyard.

"That sounds fun," Imogen said. Playing outside would wear both puppy and child out. "What games will you play? Fetch? Tag?"

"I want to play house," Ellery declared. She shoveled in several forkfuls of pancake before dashing off to the living room and returning with a flyer from a toy store. She flipped through it and found a plastic playhouse. "Daddy, can I have one of these?" She shoved the picture across the table.

The brightly colored plastic house was meant for toddlers, not for girls who were going to be in the first grade come fall. Ellery would be almost too tall for it already.

"One of those?" Patrick's tone was doubtful. "I don't know, kiddo. They're cheaply made and bad for the—"

Imogen nudged his foot under the table. When he looked at her, she tried her best to convey that he wasn't taking the right approach. Her guess was that Ellery had long wanted a playhouse and been denied it. Imogen's heart went out to the girl.

After a moment's pause, Patrick tried a different tack. "If you want a playhouse, I could build you a better one out of wood," he said.

"Could you?" Ellery's face lit up like a Christmas tree, and she threw her arms around his neck. "I'll help."

Patrick's face softened as he hugged his little girl. Imogen bit back a sigh. There was something undeniably sexy about a man who loved his child. Not that Patrick had any trouble looking sexy. He had

yesterday in his uniform, and last night when they talked, and…
whoa. That was a dangerous train of thought.

"Let's go to the store and get the supplies," Patrick said as he ate the
rest of his breakfast.

"Today?" Imogen tuned back in to the conversation. It seemed once
Patrick decided to do something, he did it *now*.

"Sure. We don't have any other plans," he said. "We'll clean up the
kitchen and go."

An hour later, Imogen felt as if she were riding a skateboard over
rocks. It seemed to be her job to maintain some sort of balance
between a practical, no-nonsense father and Ellery's desire for all that
was glitter, hearts, and rainbows. They debated the style until they
finally compromised on one that had solid construction and ginger-
bread trim. Something for everyone, Imogen had declared after a
fifteen-minute standoff.

After settling on the design and purchasing a kit and paint (interior
and exterior) from the home improvement store, they moved on to a
fabric shop for material to make curtains, pillows, and a cover for a
window seat. Making the selections took time, and Imogen could see
Patrick's patience wearing thin. She could guess that he wanted to get
home to build.

"You sure we can do this in a day?" she asked after they returned
home and hauled their purchases to the backyard. She'd put the fabric
in the house. That was her project for the next day.

"No problem." He grinned at her. "I didn't specify when the day
ended, exactly, but starting with a kit will cut some time off."

"I want to help," Ellery said, wielding a kid-sized hammer Patrick had
purchased for her. She had a tool belt and a hard hat to go with it.
"Where do we start?"

"The first task is to build the floor," Patrick said. Working together, they framed a square that would become the floor and began laying boards across it.

"Ouch!" Ellery shrieked as they were nailing the last board down. She held her thumb, tears welling in her eyes.

"Uh-oh." Patrick quickly gathered her up and inspected the injured thumb. He gave it a kiss. "There, is that a little better? I think it's going to be okay."

"I'm not very good at hammering," Ellery said. "Can I have another job?"

Patrick shot Imogen a pleading look. They were getting good at silent communication.

"Can you handle two jobs?" Imogen asked, getting an immediate nod from Ellery. "Okay, then. First, we need someone to run in the house for snacks. I'm getting hungry. How about some animal crackers?"

"I'm hungry, too," Ellery said and took off toward the back door.

"You're amazing," Patrick said, giving Imogen a smile so warm it went straight through her. "What's task number two, and will it keep her busy?"

"I've got this," Imogen promised him. "Don't worry."

When Ellery returned with the container of animal crackers, they sat at the picnic table and ate, enjoying the sunshine. The girl couldn't stay still for long, though. She jumped up, demanding, "Now what?"

"Mr. Bubblesworth is feeling left out," Imogen said, her voice very serious. They'd tied the dog to a sturdy tree in the yard, but he desperately wanted to play. "Can you entertain him?"

Ellery answered by dashing off to be with the puppy.

"Good work. I give it an hour and they'll both be so worn out they'll be asleep," Patrick said. "Time for us to assemble the walls."

They worked together throughout the afternoon, building the walls and putting them in place. Following that, they put up the trusses for the peaked roof and added the plywood.

"I'll put the metal on the roof tomorrow," Patrick said, studying the front of the little structure. "I want to get some things finished inside so Ellery can play in there right away. Think I'll build a little porch on the front. Would she like that?" he asked as they went through the door into the playhouse.

"She'll love it." Imogen looked out the window to where Ellery was sprawled in the grass alongside Mr. Bubblesworth. The girl was making a chain of dandelions and seemed perfectly content.

"Hand me that latch, would you?" Patrick finished hanging the door and bumped into her when he turned. "Sorry."

"Are you?" she asked, letting herself flirt a little. It had been fun working with him because it helped them establish a relationship of sorts. And she liked his company. A lot. "We've built a house together, just like a real married couple."

He pulled her closer to him. "If we're playing the married game, I think I should kiss you to celebrate our accomplishment."

Before she could respond, his arms went around her waist. Every kiss had a mood. Last night's kiss was a slow burn that could have developed into a forest fire. Today's was playful and fun. She liked both versions and wondered how many other kinds they could share. They separated in time to see Ellery shoot past the window, headed toward the house.

"Where's she going?" Imogen asked, stepping out of the playhouse. A minute later, Ellery returned with Todd, who was carrying a big bouquet of roses and lilies. "Hi, Todd. Are these from you?"

"Sorry, I can't take credit for the flowers. They were sitting on the porch." He placed them on the picnic table. "I came by to congratulate the two of you on your wedding."

"Thanks." Patrick reached out and shook hands with his brother.

"I hope you'll be happy together," Todd added, kissing her on the cheek.

"I appreciate that," Imogen said. She'd wondered why Patrick hadn't invited his brother to their wedding, but she hadn't interfered. It was Patrick's decision, and the wedding had been special and intimate with just the three of them.

"Come see my playhouse." Ellery took Todd's hand and pulled him toward the half-finished building.

"Do you have a secret admirer?" Patrick pointed to the flowers.

"I don't know." She plucked the card from the arrangement. *Imogen Mendel Nelson* was printed across the envelope. Someone knew she was married. Odd, since she'd told none of her friends. Patrick came to stand next to her, his hand on the small of her back. This felt off, and he must have sensed that as well.

"Open it," he said.

She broke the seal and pulled a small card from the envelope. A message was written in neat print. *Congratulations on your marriage, but remember we know where you're at. Best of luck in your future.* There was no signature or name at the end.

Imogen felt a shiver go down her spine, and only Patrick's warm hand on her back kept her from physically shaking. "It must be from my handler," she said, quietly, so Ellery and Todd didn't hear.

"What makes you think that?" Everything about him was tense, ready to pounce.

"He's a creep, but I had to tell him where I'd be living." She'd met the man just twice and hadn't been impressed. Their phone conversations more recently had cemented that opinion. "He probably thinks this is funny."

Patrick frowned, and she wondered if his mind, like hers, was running through worst-case scenarios. The flowers and the note could be from Grant's dad or someone working on his behalf. But even if they were, what could she do about it? The authorities would just tell her to report the problem to her handler, but he was the last person she felt she could trust.

11

The next morning, Patrick carried Imogen's sewing machine out to the picnic table, strung an extension cord from the garage to power it, and assumed his job was done. Imogen and Ellery were in charge of decorating the playhouse. That wasn't his world. While they made the playhouse pretty, he planned to get some yard work done. He'd made it almost to the garage to get the mower when Ellery's voice called him back.

Now what? He wanted to yell, but he clamped down on that. Ellery wanted his attention, and that was a good thing. So he turned back.

"We need curtain rods," his daughter announced. "I want fancy ones."

"Fancy ones?" He gave Imogen a perplexed look. Weren't curtain rods all the same?

"She means with finials on the ends," she explained. "Like the ones in your living room."

Huh? He had fancy curtain rods. That was news to him. He'd have to go look. "Okay. Where do I buy those?"

"The home improvement store should have a good selection," Imogen said. "Take Ellery with you so she can pick out ones she likes."

"Aren't you coming?"

Imogen shook her head. "I'm making the cushion cover for the window seat."

He wanted to beg her to come along on the trip to the store, but she'd been tense all morning. The flowers and the note yesterday had gotten under her skin. She'd hardly spoken a word during dinner and had gone to bed early, claiming she was tired. She probably was, after a day of building, but he'd like her to confide in him.

He didn't see the note as being that big a deal. So what if someone knew she was married and living with him? If anything, that might deter someone from coming after her. She wasn't alone anymore, and he had the skills to protect her. He thought she understood that.

"Sure," he said, taking Ellery's hand. "Let's go get your fancy curtain rods."

By the time they reached the store, he wanted to call a time out. Ellery had talked nonstop in the car, which was nothing unusual for her, but her excitement about the playhouse had the pitch of her voice rising. The shrillness grated on his nerves.

Things didn't improve once they got inside, where Ellery darted away from him and he nearly lost her. Once he got her to the right aisle, it took a full fifteen minutes for her to select the perfect knobs for her curtain rods. Trying to hurry her along did nothing other than push her closer to having the kind of tantrum he'd seen on other days. Thankfully he'd wised up about that in time to avoid a meltdown. Letting her have her way was probably the wrong approach, but he didn't know the right one. He had some things to learn about being a father —Imogen had been correct about that. So he stood in the aisle as patiently as he could while Ellery decided between three "finalists" that all looked essentially the same to him.

When they finally got back home, he hoped to be relieved of duty, but instead he had to hang the rods after Ellery changed her mind over and over about their exact height. Following that, he painted the door of the white playhouse bright pink, which would have been easy without Ellery's help. No such luck.

"Sorry, Daddy," Ellery said, backing away after she put a stripe of pink paint across his shirt.

"It's okay," he said, controlling the curse that came to his lips. He used a paper towel to wipe off the excess. "No worries."

"Don't you think this is the prettiest color pink?"

"It's great." Where the hell was Imogen? His eyes went to her. She was running fabric through the sewing machine. When she finished the seam, she glanced up, catching his eye.

"You look good in pink," she called, a smile on her face. The first one he'd seen since yesterday.

"Can we paint the window frames pink, too?" Ellery asked, tipping her face up to his in what he'd decided to call her "adorable" look. She used it when she wanted her way. That might become a problem, but it was also irresistible.

Pink around the windows would look garish as hell, but why not? "Okay. Pink it is."

After finishing the door, they moved on to the window frames, which required more skill. Patrick spent most of his time catching drips before they ran down the white. It was fine, he told himself. He was spending time with his daughter, forming connections... but Jesus, this would be an easier task by himself.

By late afternoon, he'd painted, hung curtains, fetched decorative stuff from the house, and was in the garage rebuilding the window seat to Ellery's specifications. He was so over this project. Was this what his life was going to be like for the next fifteen years?

He needed to talk to another guy, so he reached for his phone, dialing Anderson without thinking. And then it hit him. His SEAL teammate was already out on another mission and couldn't be reached.

"Damn," Patrick swore, feeling a brief wave of jealousy. Anderson was doing what they were trained to do. Patrick had no idea what his mission was, but he imagined it was a hell of a lot more interesting than hanging curtains.

He tried Todd next, but it went to voicemail.

He eyed his pickup. He could get in and start driving, leave Imogen to deal for a while. He felt bad considering it, but Ellery and her demands were driving him to distraction. When he'd put the last screw in the window seat, he looked at his truck again. Just a couple hours to himself. That's all he was asking.

He fingered the keys in his jeans pocket, temptation almost getting the better of him. Then he stopped himself. Rachel had abandoned Ellery, allowing her to be turned over to foster care. Was he as poor a father as Rachel had been a mother?

Shit, he didn't want to be that, but was he for even thinking of leaving?

"I think you deserve this." Imogen held out a beer. He'd been so caught up in his own thoughts that he hadn't heard her enter the garage.

"Thanks," he said, his tone gruff. He took the bottle, popped the cap off, and took a long drink.

"Let's take a walk," she said, holding up the dog leash. "Mr. Bubblesworth could do with some exercise. And we could both do with some time away from this project." She gestured to the window seat on his workbench.

"What about Ellery?" he asked, since Imogen appeared to be alone.

"She was watching Discovery Family Channel and fell asleep on the couch. She'll be fine for a little while if we stay within earshot. Come on." Imogen led the way into the backyard and snapped the leash on Mr. B, and together they headed for the road.

Without discussing it, they walked toward the wooded area, stopping occasionally for the dog to sniff the ground. Mr. B was doing better on the leash. They didn't talk, and Patrick was thankful for the quiet. He'd always found his home to be peaceful, and maybe that was the problem. The alone time that he always sought after a mission was no more. Not with Ellery and Imogen living in his house. He'd have to get used to it, and he would, once they got into some sort of routine.

"Ellery's a tough taskmaster," Imogen said after several minutes of silence. "She had a vision for her playhouse, though, I've got to give her credit for that."

"Damn near wore us out creating it," he agreed ruefully.

"I think she's had very little that she could call her own," Imogen said after another pause. "Maybe very little control over herself or her environment."

Patrick felt a wash of guilt at the words, because they were true. Ellery wasn't deprived, exactly, but she was hungry for attention and love. He could give her those things, but child-rearing was more challenging than he'd thought it would be. Now he could understand the CPS committee's reluctance to grant him full custody. They must have seen that he wasn't ready.

"I almost got in my truck and drove off today," he said and waited for Imogen's judgment. He deserved it.

"I think all parents feel like that at some point." They reached where the road dead-ended in the woods and turned back.

"Do they?" That was hard to believe. He'd seen some of his teammates with their kids. None of them ever looked like they were going to bolt. The flaw must be in him. "Not sure I'm cut out for this. I never know what to expect from Ellery, and she can be… demanding." He hated to say that about his own daughter, but it was true.

"She can be. Her situation—"

"Which is my fault," he said, cutting Imogen off before she could make excuses for him. "If I'd taken more responsibility for her years ago, things would be different."

"You're taking responsibility now," Imogen replied. "It's more than a lot of people would do. You're doing everything you can now to make her feel safe and happy. And you're doing the same for me. Don't be so hard on yourself."

"I don't like failing," he admitted. It wasn't in his nature. Some things in his life had come easy to him, others he'd worked his ass off for, but he'd always found success. He wasn't sure he could do that as a parent.

"You aren't going to fail. Trust me on that," she said.

"I don't know." He had a lot of doubts about this.

"Tell me this," she said. "If you had gotten in your truck and driven off, would you have come back?"

"Of course I would." His answer was instant.

Imogen stepped in front of him, and Mr. B put his butt on the pavement. When Patrick stopped, she put her hands on his shoulders and kept her gaze steady on him. "All parents need a break sometimes. You shouldn't feel bad about that. The point is that you'd come back, that you'd *want* to come back." Without another word, she pulled him in for a hug of comfort. "You'll be fine," she said, letting him go after a minute. "We'll be fine. Let's go back to the house."

She resumed walking, but this time she took his hand. Her hug and the feel of her fingers in his were comforting and reassuring. They also reminded him of the attraction that simmered between them whenever they touched… which he was thinking more and more about acting on.

They made their way back to the house and crept in so as not to disturb Ellery, who was still sleeping on the couch. Imogen released Mr. B, who disappeared into the kitchen. Seconds later, they heard him drinking noisily from his water bowl.

"Thanks," he whispered, drawing Imogen to him until their bodies were touching. "You make everything better."

Her eyes widened in surprise. Maybe she hadn't expected such blunt honesty from him, but he saw no reason to keep his gratitude—and attraction—a secret. She hadn't objected to their previous kisses, so he ran a finger along her jawline and guided her mouth to his. This kiss was different from the beginning. She opened to him immediately. Their tongues met in an impromptu dance of advance and retreat, revealing the heat that flared easily between them.

He pressed her closer so he could feel her breasts against his chest, and her arms tightened around him, her fingers kneading the skin of his back. She wanted this as much as he did. His lips moved to kiss a line down her long neck and back up. His hands were sliding under the edge of her T-shirt, just beginning to touch warm, smooth skin, when Ellery stirred on the couch. Imogen stilled in his arms. Her eyes, still heavy with desire, opened.

Reluctantly, he let her go.

12

"What are we doing today?" Ellery asked the same question she did over breakfast every morning.

"Check the board," Patrick said. He poured coffee for Imogen and himself and brought the cups to the table.

"Thanks." Imogen accepted the mug, appreciating his thoughtfulness… among other things. They were cautious never to be too affectionate in front of Ellery, but in the rare moments when she was occupied, there were wonderful stolen kisses. Imogen knew she shouldn't get used to any of this, but each day she felt more drawn to him.

"P-O-O-L," Ellery read from the board that listed the day's activities. "The pool. Again?"

Imogen liked that Ellery got to practice her reading, but the real reason for the posted schedule was Patrick's love of structure. Conveniently, structure worked well for children. In the past days they had settled into a comfortable routine. Imogen was glad not to be in charge for a change. From September to May she had to make all the decisions in her classroom, so it was nice to leave that to someone else for a while. Patrick consulted her, but she hadn't found any reason to object to his plans, so she'd happily gone along with them. As a matter of fact, she was surprisingly happy in her temporary marriage. For the first time in nearly a year, she felt safe. The threatening phone calls still came in waves, none for a few days and then a barrage, but the threat felt more distant. She realized that was naïve thinking, but she hated to dwell on the negative.

"I don't want to go," Ellery said, returning to the table. Her bottom lip came out in a stubborn pout, which Imogen and Patrick had learned to recognize as a warning sign of her behavior becoming problematic.

"Why not?" Patrick asked, his tone neutral. "The water will feel good today. It's going to be a hot one."

"They're not nice to me at the pool." Ellery's lip started to tremble.

"Who wasn't nice to you?" Patrick looked from Ellery to Imogen.

"Tell your dad what happened," Imogen encouraged softly.

"Can you tell him?" Tears started brimming in the girl's eyes, and Imogen took pity on her.

"Yesterday when we went without you," Imogen told Patrick, "the pool manager said that Ellery was too big for the wading pool. It's meant for kids under the age of five."

"So? Use the main pool." He clearly didn't understand what the big deal was, but he hadn't seen Ellery's expression.

"She wouldn't. It made her *uncomfortable*," Imogen said, trying to phrase it gently. Ellery had flatly refused to dip a toe in the big pool, even when Imogen offered to go in with her. Recognizing fear when she saw it, Imogen decided not to force the girl, so they'd packed up their things and left. Patrick hadn't gotten home until late in the evening after a day helping a friend with a building project, so they hadn't told him.

"Honey, are you scared of the bigger pool?" Patrick asked, and Ellery nodded. A perplexed expression passed over his face. He was probably never afraid of anything. Would he understand his daughter's fear? To his credit, when he spoke again, his words were carefully chosen. "Water should be respected but not feared."

"What if I go under and can't come back up?" The girl's voice was small, lacking her usual bravado.

"That's why you should learn how to swim," Patrick explained, "so that doesn't happen. If you go under, you'll know how to get back to the surface."

Ellery's face scrunched up as if she were considering the idea. "Maybe," she finally said.

"Why don't you think about it for a little while?" Imogen suggested.

"Okay. I'm going to my house." Ellery went out the back door. In the time since the playhouse had been completed, they'd heard her utter that sentence often. She loved her little house in the backyard, and Imogen suspected it was because it was the first big thing Ellery had asked for and gotten.

Patrick pulled his phone out and started scrolling through pages.

"What are you doing?" she asked as she gathered up the breakfast dishes.

"Setting up swim lessons for her." His tone was matter-of-fact.

"What? She may not want to take lessons." Imogen could sympathize. She'd go in the pool, but it wasn't her favorite activity, either. Whenever she'd visited the ocean, she'd stuck to wading along the shore. Ellery's fears were legitimate.

"I'm a SEAL." Patrick looked her in the eye. "We're trained to practically live in the water. There's no reason to be scared of it."

"But that's you, the naval officer," Imogen argued. "You're not a six-year-old kid."

"She has to learn to swim," he said flatly, and Imogen bit her lip to keep from arguing. She thought he was being unreasonable about this, but she had to remember… his kid, his choice. She didn't have to like it, though. He met her eyes, seeming to understand her thoughts. "It'll be all right, Imogen. I'll make sure she doesn't get thrown in the deep end—literally or otherwise. There have to be classes for kids her age. Yep, here we go." He'd returned his attention to his phone. "The city offers them. I'm signing her up. She'll be swimming like a fish in no time."

Fortunately, when Ellery returned from her playhouse a little while later, she'd made up her mind to try to learn to swim, and Patrick let her maintain the illusion that it had been her choice.

Two lessons later, Ellery was proving her dad right. She seemed well on her way to learning to swim and getting over her fear of water.

The first lesson had been touch and go until a boy from her kindergarten class showed up. Not wanting to look bad in front of a classmate, Ellery had gotten in the water and cooperated with the lifeguard who was giving instructions.

During the second lesson, Imogen and Patrick lounged by the pool, watching Ellery play a game where she had to swim through a hoop held by the instructor. The idea was to get the kids more comfortable in the water. Ellery didn't like getting her face wet to pass through the hoop, but she was doing it.

"You were right," Imogen said to Patrick over the sounds of splashing and laughter. "Although I do wonder why you didn't just teach her yourself."

"I'm a doer, not a teacher," Patrick said. "I can give orders with the best of them, but explaining how to do something isn't my thing." He leaned back, looking comfortable in the lounge chair. "Besides, it's never a good idea to teach someone who's so close to you."

"Really?" she asked, surprised by his statement. That wasn't her philosophy at all. "I've always thought that knowing and loving someone made it easier to teach them."

"It's obvious that you care for your students," he said, his eyes meeting hers, "so that must work for you."

"It does." She was going to say more, but Ellery climbed from the pool and dashed toward them, flinging droplets as she went. She grabbed her father's arm and tried to pull him back toward the water.

For a second, Imogen wasn't sure what he would do. Sometimes he reacted badly to spontaneous behavior, but not this time. He scooped up his wet daughter and jumped into the pool holding her. Imogen laughed, glad that he'd worn swim trunks and a T-shirt to the lesson or it would have been a soggy drive home.

Since the class was over and other kids were leaving, there was plenty of space in the pool for dad and daughter to play. They splashed each other, and Patrick dove underwater to grab Ellery's legs and make her squeal. He seemed to know how much to do to make Ellery laugh without frightening her. After a few minutes, Patrick just held his daughter and floated in the water with her.

Imogen wanted to take a picture to preserve the intimate moment. Patrick and Ellery were understanding each other better, and the love she'd seen between them from the beginning was apparent so often now.

Imogen had wondered if she'd feel uncomfortable as the two of them grew closer, since she was on the outside to a certain extent—but she wasn't. She was glad for them, glad they'd have a relationship long after she was out of their lives. The thought of being disconnected from them in the future made her sad, but that was the arrangement she'd agreed to.

Suddenly, Ellery giggled and began yanking her dad's shirt up around his shoulders in an attempt to trap him in the material. Clever little girl, trying to give herself the advantage, Imogen thought as she watched Patrick struggle with the wet fabric. When he couldn't resettle it, he pulled it off, then immediately tried to put the shirt back on. Why, she wondered. His body was first-rate. He was standing in the pool now, and she could see his tatted-up chest and ripped abs above the waterline.

"Let me get my shirt back on," he said to Ellery, his voice unexpectedly sharp as she dodged around, trying to splash him.

Giving up on the sodden shirt, Patrick tossed it on the pool deck and backed toward the edge. He'd caught Ellery in front of him and was holding her at arm's length, making no response to her playful actions as he had just moments earlier. Imogen couldn't understand his behavior. She stood up and walked to the pool, freezing when she caught a glimpse of his exposed back and realized what the problem was. Deep scars sliced across his skin from shoulder to shoulder; a more jagged one ran alongside his spine, then veered to one side. Her breath left her body in a gush. She'd known he was a soldier, risking his life for his country, but she hadn't thought of the danger he must have faced so often until that moment.

She shook herself back into action and rushed to grab two towels, understanding now why he wouldn't let Ellery behind him and so desperately wanted to cover himself. Even a child would understand that something awful had happened to him. When she reached him,

Imogen took another, closer look. She couldn't stop herself. Some of the scars were older, white and ridged; some were red, indicating more-recent trauma. All were symbols of the violence and pain he'd endured. She tore her gaze away from him to address Ellery.

"Come on, sweetie. Time to get out of the water. Pretty soon, you're going to shrivel up." She kept her tone light so as not to alarm the girl. "And we've got other things to do today. Remember Mr. Bubblesworth's visit to the veterinarian." The appointment wasn't for hours, but it worked as a distraction.

"Oh, right." Ellery's attention immediately shifted, and she headed for the ladder and got out of the pool.

"Here, dry yourself off." Imogen met the girl at the ladder and wrapped her in an oversized towel from her head to her toes.

While Ellery was busy wringing out her hair, Imogen handed the second towel to Patrick.

"Thanks," he grunted, putting it around him and not seeming to care that it dragged in the pool. He didn't look up or meet her eyes.

Surely he wasn't ashamed of the scars? No, she realized in the next instant, that wasn't it. He didn't want her pity or compassion. Despite the sunshine, she felt a chill go through her, but her next instinct was to reach out to him and soothe the man under the scar tissue. She stopped herself, not sure he'd welcome the attention. Something else was clear to her, though. He would be a dangerous man to care for deeply, because the reality of what he did—the risks he ran—would always be there between them.

And she'd let herself begin to care for him.

She turned away, not knowing what to say, and kept Ellery busy while he wrung out his shirt and got it on.

13

———————

The sun was just setting when Patrick stepped into the backyard with Mr. B. The dog needed to do his business before bed, and Patrick was in the habit of walking the perimeter of his property every evening. Not that he expected trouble, but he had people in his life to protect now.

Protect from everything, even his scars. He'd kept his shirt on at all times, even in the sweltering heat of a South Carolina summer, since he wasn't ready to show Ellery the result of his experiences as a SEAL. And he wouldn't be for a long damn time. He hadn't wanted Imogen to see, either. He'd been so damn careful since they'd married to stay covered up.

Thank God for her quick thinking at the pool, but he couldn't assess her reaction. Was she repulsed, or had that been sorrow in her eyes? She'd acted for the rest of the day as though nothing had happened, but things were off kilter between them. Her behavior was too bright, verging on brittle.

He whistled for Mr. B to return to him. His doubts about the dog had been somewhat unfounded. He was still an oversized, undisciplined puppy for the most part, but he'd shown he was capable of learning basic commands.

"You're a good boy." Patrick scratched the dog's head, giving him attention and praise as a reward for coming when called. Dogs were easy to manage, straightforward. Once they got in the house, Mr. B went upstairs to Ellery's room, where he'd snooze until morning. A much more difficult task awaited Patrick.

He needed to talk to Imogen now that Ellery was in bed. Patrick headed for the living room. The tone of a male voice reached him first. Did they have a visitor? But when he entered, he saw Imogen holding her phone and listening to her messages. From the look on her face, they were more threats. He paused to listen to the words now that he was closer. He didn't like what he heard.

"You'll regret it if you testify."

"You're a pretty girl. I'll bet we can find a good use for you."

Each threat was followed by a string of profanity and further suggestions of what they were willing to do to her. Her skin was pale, almost ghostly, and she had her eyes closed as if that could shut out some of the horror.

"Why do you listen to those?" Patrick asked, making her jump. "Just delete them."

She tapped a button on her phone, cutting off the vulgar message. "I can't help it," she said. "I keep thinking that the callers will do something to identify themselves. And what if I miss that? Or what if they say something else that could be incriminating, and I could take additional evidence to the district attorney?" She tossed her phone onto the coffee table. "I know it's not healthy, but it's kind of an obsession that I can't break."

Or was it a manifestation of her fear? He'd married her partly to put her mind at rest, but had he? He had to know. "Do you trust me to keep you safe?" he asked.

"I do… but I'm still scared. I can't help that." She was almost gasping for air. He crossed the room quickly and took her hand.

"Breathe, sweetheart," he said and watched her take in a long breath and let it out slowly. After a moment, she seemed to settle.

"Sorry," she said. "I don't mean to get panicky, but this isn't my life. I'm not made to face danger like you do. Patrick, your back…"

"It's healed," he said, shrugging off her concern. He didn't want this to be about him or his past.

"But it must have been horribly painful." Her expression started to crack, and he feared she'd cry. Not over him, please, not over him.

"Shush," he said softly. "I'm fine now." Putting his arms around her, he pressed her face into his shoulder and ran his hands in long strokes down her back.

"But you'll go on another mission," she said, her voice muffled against him, "and it could happen again."

Did she care for him? Part of him wanted her to, but he couldn't let himself feel that way. He had no need to be coddled, by her or anyone else. He'd understood that as a kid, when his mom walked out on the family. His years of leading others on missions had reinforced it. His job was to protect others, like he was trying to do for her.

"I'm here now," he said, dropping a kiss on her hair.

She moved her arms, which had been trapped between them, and slid them around his waist. They'd been this close before, but this embrace felt different, more intimate than the kisses they'd shared since their wedding day. As much as he wanted her, he'd held back, not wanting to complicate an already complicated situation. But maybe he'd been thinking about it wrong. Maybe she needed more from him.

He bent his head over hers. Maybe he needed more from her, too. It was a frightening thought, but he couldn't deny it. And they were married—for now—and exclusive to each other. He knew he was trying to justify his desire for her. Before he could talk himself out of making love to her, she kissed the side of his neck, sending an electric current through him.

He groaned when her lips traveled to his jaw in little, biting kisses. God, that felt good. His powers of resistance were strong, but not against her. He found her mouth, kissing her with all the desire he'd been keeping leashed. She responded instantly, letting him know what she wanted as well, but he needed her to say the words.

He broke the kiss, putting space between their bodies so they could both think. The color had returned to her face, and her lips were already swollen from kissing. Her expression was soft, almost loving, and he wanted her so much.

"If we don't stop, we'll end up in bed together," he forced himself to say. "Are you sure that's what you want?"

She nodded. "You?"

He couldn't believe she had to ask. "Hell, yes."

A tiny smile appeared on her face. "Well, I guess it's about time we celebrated our wedding night, then."

They came back together, their kiss dangerous and seductive now. Her hands went under his shirt, and she started to lift the fabric up, but he stopped her. "Not here," he panted. "Bed." Without bothering with more words, he scooped her up and headed for the stairs. In her bedroom he put her on her feet. "I'll be right back."

He crossed the hall, peeking in on Ellery and Mr. B. They were both sound asleep, so he shut the bedroom door. Next, he went to his room for the condoms in his drawer. He grabbed one but decided that wasn't going to be enough. He carried the box back to the master bedroom.

He stopped cold in the doorway. Imogen had stripped off her tank top and shorts, leaving her in a lacy bra and thong. She was beautiful, her body both soft and muscled. His dick hardened in anticipation. She was beautiful, and she was his, at least for now.

Her eyes dropped to the box in his hand. "Feeling ambitious?" she asked. Her smile was pure seduction as she came toward him. To his disappointment, she walked around him, and he almost panicked before he realized she was simply closing the bedroom door. She could still think, apparently. He was past rational thought. He reached out for her, but she evaded his grip and took the box from him.

"We better put these somewhere handy," she said, crossing the room to place the condoms on the nightstand. There was a slight blush on her cheeks, revealing that she wasn't quite the seductress she was playing the part of, but her voice was clear as she said, "Come make love to me, Patrick."

He didn't have to be told twice. He crossed to where she stood by the bed in three strides and put his hands on her bare waist. He slid his palms down to cup her butt cheeks. They were perfect little handfuls. And the thong and bra were enticing, but he wanted them gone. He hooked his fingers under the edges of her panties and pushed them down until they dropped soundlessly to the floor.

He put a kiss on the soft curve of each breast as he unsnapped her bra. She wriggled out of it, then gasped when he licked her left nipple, quickly bringing it to a point so he could tease it with his lips. He repeated his actions on the other side, listening to her breathing change as she became more excited. His fingers skimmed down her stomach to the dark hair between her thighs.

"I wasn't sure if you were really a blonde," he said as his fingers delved into her silky wetness.

"Now you know I'm not," she whispered. "Does that change anything?"

He pushed a finger inside her, pleased when he felt a shiver go through her. "Not at all. I think it's time we got on the bed." Reluctantly, he removed his hand from between her thighs and eased her onto the mattress, then shed his clothes. Her hazel eyes blazed as they swept down his body. "I hope you don't mind tattoos and scars."

"All part of who you are," she said as he moved to settle himself above her. "The muscles and strength are you, too." With her fingertip, she drew a line from his throat to his navel, where she paused for a heartbeat before wrapping her hand around his dick. She stroked up the length and rubbed her thumb over the tip. He sucked in a breath. "Again?" She didn't wait for his answer as she repeated the action.

He couldn't take that a third time, not without coming in her hand, so he lowered himself onto her, distracting her with a kiss. But his action worked against him as the kiss deepened and he listened to her little sounds of pleasure. When she arched her body up, thrusting her hips against his, he knew he couldn't wait any longer. With one last nip at her lips, he rolled away from her and reached for a condom.

He rolled it on quickly and came back to her, hovering just above her, their bodies not quite touching. He wanted to savor the moment, but he also desperately wanted to be inside her. When she put her hands on his shoulders and spread her legs for him, he couldn't wait a second longer. Lowering himself down, he thrust into her tight heat. He stilled, letting himself enjoy the velvety feel of her, but when she tightened her internal muscles around him, he had to respond.

He kissed her lips, her neck, her breasts as their bodies moved together in a rhythm that was uniquely theirs. He teased her with his fingers, wanting to ensure she was feeling the same heat he was. He could feel the tension in her body, and the moment when it unraveled, sending her into an orgasm.

"Oh, Patrick," she whimpered, her head tilted back in ecstasy.

He thrust once more into her, giving up any control he'd had and letting himself come inside her. When the waves of his orgasm ended, he rolled onto his back and pulled her on top of him. She lay sprawled on him as he continued to move his hands over her body. He didn't think he'd ever want to stop touching her.

14

———————

"I'll be back to pick you up when you're done." Patrick gave Ellery a quick hug and sent her through the gate to the outdoor swimming pool with her swim instructor. He lingered a moment to watch, but it was clear that she was fine with being left at the pool. She had an individual lesson followed by a group lesson, giving him ninety minutes. Since it was a ten-minute drive home, that gave him time for a quickie with Imogen before he had to return.

He couldn't keep the grin off his face when he got in the truck to return home. The night before with Imogen had been amazing. He wanted a repeat of that and a whole lot more. He walked inside and found Imogen in the living room, lounging on the couch with a book in her hands.

"I didn't expect you home," she said, looking up with a smile.

"I thought we might enjoy some kid-free time." He dropped to his knees on the floor next to her.

"Whatever for?" She batted her eyelashes at him, all with innocence.

"For this." He skimmed his hand over her breast as he kissed her. Her response was immediate, ramping up his own desire. A moment later he was on the couch next to her, their bodies glued together.

"Wait," she said, pushing gently at his chest. "I almost forgot. I'd just put Mr. Bubblesworth in the backyard when you came home. I'd better get him before we…"

"Before we… what?" he challenged.

"Before I rip your clothes off you and ride you right here on the living room floor," she said brazenly, but a blush followed the daring words.

He rolled off her immediately and stretched out on the floor. "Hurry back." Her description of what would happen between them wasn't what he'd expect a kindergarten teacher to say, but she'd proved last night that she had plenty of passion in her. She hopped up, and he couldn't resist running his hand up her sexy bare leg. He got several inches above her knee before she brushed his fingers away and headed for the kitchen.

He put his hands behind his head, letting his imagination take over. He was thinking about how she'd unzip his shorts and—

A scream and Mr. B's furious barking had him launching himself off the floor and bolting toward the noise.

"Get out!" Imogen's voice cut through the air as Patrick slid into the kitchen and nearly collided with her. A man dressed in all black with a ski mask covering his face stood in the back door with Imogen's laptop in his hands and Mr. B's teeth clamped around one leg. The panic in his eyes was almost comical as he kicked and struggled to free himself from the dog.

Mr. B wasn't letting go, so the man dropped the laptop and half fell out the back door with the dog still attached to him. Once outside, he started running toward the gate. Mr. B. stayed with him. Patrick was headed for the door, ready for the chase, when he saw Imogen's ashen face. She was visibly shaking. He turned back to her, taking her hand and guiding her to a kitchen chair.

"It's okay. You're okay," he said, quickly.

"Mr. Bubblesworth," she said, sounding panicked. "Is he okay? Did that man hurt him?"

"No idea. I'm going after them. Lock the door behind me." He was less concerned about the dog's welfare than he was about the person who'd broken into his home. Mr. B seemed to be able to hold his own.

"Be careful." A little color returned to her face, so he gave her hand a last squeeze and left the house. Outside, he circled to the front. He hadn't heard a car, so whoever this was had been on foot. He paused to listen and heard a bark in the direction of the woods.

He took off at a run, giving the intruder some credit for being able to move quickly even with Mr. B in tow. But the guy was no good at covering his tracks. Broken branches showed where he'd ducked off the road.

Patrick slowed his pace and opened his senses as he entered the woods. He worked methodically, finding more damaged branches and crushed undergrowth, all the while keeping his ears tuned to the sounds of the dog's barks. The woods, with the trees in full leaf, dampened and distorted sounds, so following the barks alone wasn't enough. Patrick had gone a quarter mile into the woods when the barks were suddenly getting closer. Had the intruder doubled back?

Patrick hunkered down behind a large tree and waited. He heard the whine of a dog, but no sound of a man moving. Feeling confident that Mr. B was alone, Patrick stepped out of his hiding place and the dog trotted toward him alone.

"Wish you could talk, buddy," Patrick said, scratching at Mr. B's ears. "I'm willing to bet he had a car on the other road." A country road ran along the opposite side of the woods. If Patrick were going to plan an attack on his home, he'd have parked there, too. Someone had thought about this. Planned it. But who?

"Let's head back." With the dog next to him, he moved quickly back through the woods to his house. When they neared it, the front door flew open and Imogen darted out.

"You're both safe," she said, running up to them. She seemed divided about who to hug first, so she gripped Patrick's hand and dropped to her knees to wrap her other arm around Mr. B. The panting dog soaked up the attention and would have gotten a belly rub if Patrick hadn't pulled Imogen to her feet.

"We need to report this to the police." He'd decided that on the way back but knew he'd have to convince her.

"No," she said with a firm shake of her head. "I'm sure it was—"

"Not random. You know that," he said. "Someone must have been watching the house and saw me leave, but he didn't realize I was coming back. He intended to enter when you were alone. We can't let that go." He held her eyes with his. "I can't let that go." The thought that the intruder might have caught her reading on the couch in an otherwise empty house made his blood boil.

"But getting the police involved..." Her defenses were breaking down, so he kept at it.

"It needs to go on record, and while they're here, you can tell them about the threatening messages you've gotten." Her eyes flashed to his. She didn't like that, but he continued. "It's all part of the harassment, and it's being orchestrated by someone."

"But we don't know who, so what good will it do?" she asked.

"Documentation," Patrick insisted. The civilian world wasn't his area of expertise, but he knew that was important. "You'll need proof once these guys are caught. Involving the police is the best way to do that."

"I guess so," she agreed, still looking doubtful.

He guided her and the dog toward the house. Once they were all safely inside and he'd checked that the rest of the home was secure, he made a phone call requesting that an officer come take a report about a break-in. When he was finished, he turned to Imogen. She was sitting on the couch, absentmindedly petting Mr. B.

"Why your laptop?" he asked, remembering that the man had held it, and he hadn't been wearing gloves. The police might be able to fingerprint it, which would be good.

"I don't know." She was silent for a moment. "Maybe they're looking for what I know or my communications with the district attorney. I guess that would make sense. You know, this could have just been a crime of opportunity. An unlocked door, a laptop in sight."

"Nope." He wasn't buying it. All of his instincts pointed to the fact that this had been planned.

The police arrived minutes later, and Patrick walked the officers through the event from his perspective and showed him where the chase had led into the woods. The police were interviewing Imogen when his phone rang. He stepped out to the porch to take the call.

"Nelson," he said, not recognizing the number.

"Mr. Nelson," a young female voice responded. "This is Claudia at the pool. Was someone coming to pick up Ellery?"

Son of a bitch. Ellery. He looked at his watch. Her last lesson had ended nearly thirty minutes ago. With the events at home, he'd forgotten his child at the damn pool.

"Tell her I'll be right there," he said and hung up. He stalked to his truck, cursing himself with every foul word he knew. He'd abandoned his kid. Despite his best effort at being a parent, he'd done the unthinkable.

15

———————

"Hi, sweetie," Imogen said when Ellery and Patrick returned from the pool. She'd gotten a text from Patrick explaining why he'd dashed off. Fortunately, the police were gone before they returned, so they didn't have to explain to Ellery why the cops were at the house. "How was your lesson?"

"Okay, I guess." Ellery was sulky, but Imogen couldn't blame her for that. A child who'd been abandoned once wouldn't take being left, even for a half hour, well. "Let's have a movie night. And as a special treat, you can eat dinner in your pj's. Go on up and change."

With a fleeting glance at her father, Ellery climbed the steps. Normally, she'd be excited about watching movies with them, but she wasn't in a mood to be pacified. That was going to take some work.

Patrick waited until Ellery's bedroom door closed before he spoke. "She hates me."

"No, she's just sad." Imogen walked to him and put her arms around his neck. "Was she in any danger?"

"No," he said, clasping his hands loosely around her. "She was sitting with the lifeguards in their break room when I got there. She's refusing to talk to me, though."

"Of course she is." Imogen gave him a knowing smile. "That's how she's expressing that she's upset. We'll spoil her a bit tonight, and it'll be forgotten soon enough. Trust me on this. She won't hold a grudge."

Patrick shook his head. "I failed a basic test of parenthood. Put the child first. What would CPS say if they found out?"

"There were extenuating circumstances. They would understand," Imogen assured him. Earlier she had been upset, and Patrick had helped her. She was returning the favor now. They balanced each other pretty well, considering the unusual nature of their relationship. "Your house was invaded by a masked stranger, who ran off with our dog attached to him. Not a run-of-the-mill day."

"I liked my plan for the day better," he said softly as he moved in for a kiss, reminding her of how much more pleasantly they could have spent the afternoon.

"Rain check," she said as footsteps sounded overhead. They broke apart before Ellery came down the stairs. "You guys pick out a couple movies. I'll call for pizza and make popcorn."

Imogen went into the kitchen, keeping herself busy but listening to the conversation between father and daughter. There was tension, but it faded somewhat when Patrick agreed to a screening of *Frozen* and *Frozen II*. By the time Imogen returned to the living room, they were sitting on the couch together, waiting for her.

"Sit here." Ellery patted the couch on her other side.

When Imogen sat, Ellery cuddled into her side, pulling away from her father. Imogen didn't think the girl was punishing her dad with her actions, but rather just seeking comfort with someone more familiar. No big deal. It would pass quickly.

Throughout the evening, as they watched the movies and ate snacks, Ellery's chilliness toward her dad dissipated, and in the end, she was perfectly happy to let him tuck her into bed.

"See, it was fine," Imogen said when Patrick came back downstairs to help her clean up.

"I don't know," he said. "I think I should plan something special for her."

"You could, but it's probably not necessary." She understood his need to try, but normalcy was what Ellery craved. That was the best gift he could give her. She tried to think of a tactful and convincing way to say that.

"I'll figure it out tomorrow," Patrick said, clearly intending to go above and beyond. It wasn't her place to interfere in that, so she let it go.

"I'm headed for bed myself," she said when they'd loaded the dishwasher. His eyes met hers, and she saw the question there. Was she willing to have him in her bed a second night? You bet she was. He was her husband, after all, and one heck of a lover. "I wouldn't mind company."

He grinned at her, the first happiness she'd seen from him in hours. "I'm going to secure things for the night, and then I'll be up."

True to his word, he made her night memorable, but the next days were tense. He was trying too hard with Ellery, desperately trying to make up for what he saw as his failure. He'd set up things for them to do together: a trip to a canine rescue center so Ellery could pet the dogs, an afternoon at a pottery class where Ellery made a princess plate. He even added refinements to the playhouse, including a front porch, window boxes, and landscaping.

He invited Imogen to join them, but she declined most of the time, recognizing what he was trying to do with his father-daughter fun time. And Ellery was having fun with her dad. Who wouldn't, when he was lavishing attention on her?

But it was Imogen who scrubbed the clay from the pottery class from under Ellery's fingernails and combed the snarls out of her hair after days spent "working" on things in the backyard. As Imogen did another load of laundry, she felt a little grouchy about getting the mundane, decidedly not fun jobs associated with parenthood.

She shouldn't have complained, though, since that had been the bargain she'd made in the first place. Help him bond with his child in exchange for protection. And he was doing that part. She noticed his increased vigilance around the house. He had even installed a security system for when she was home alone. Imogen appreciated all that, but she wanted more. She wanted to be part of the family, not the glorified maid and babysitter.

She recognized the emotions churning through her, even though they'd been dormant for several years. She hadn't had a family since her parents' deaths. Longing for that was coloring her perspective, making her want things she had no right to. She slammed the lid of the washer shut and reminded herself again why she was there.

A sudden rainstorm one afternoon changed Patrick's plans for the day, leaving him without something special for Ellery to do for the first time in days. He'd improvised, taking her up to the attic to explore. Ten minutes later, the girl dashed into Imogen's bedroom, her arms full of fabric scraps.

"Can you make me a fairy costume?" Ellery said, bouncing up onto the bed. "Look at all this." She spread the fabric out around her. The variety of textiles and colors were amazing. Shiny red silk, brown tweed, a beautiful rich blue velvet, black satin that might have been part of an evening gown, the fur collar from an old coat. "And there's tons more. Come see." Ellery grabbed Imogen's hand and dragged her to the drop-down staircase.

Patrick was standing in the dimly lit attic space, studying stacks of boxes. "I think these are all fabric and craft stuff." He pointed to four boxes. One was open, its contents dragged out. That must have been the one Ellery opened first.

"Is it okay with you if I make Ellery a fairy outfit from some of this? I assume it was your grandmother's," Imogen said. A week ago she might have assumed rather than asking permission, but Patrick had become more possessive about Ellery and her time in that week, leaving a bit of tension between them. Except at night. No tension then—at least, not the unpleasant kind. But nighttime and daytime were very different things for them.

"Fine by me," he said. "I'll haul the stuff down."

Imogen set up her sewing machine on the dining room table. Since they never ate there, preferring the little kitchen table, it was safe to spread out. She was excited to have Ellery's attention for this project. They opened boxes of material, digging to the bottom and pulling out possibilities.

"This is so pretty," Ellery said, taking a piece of moss-green velvet from a box. "And this." The purple tulle had her attention next. So many choices. At first, Ellery thought she might want to be a woodland fairy in browns and greens, but shiny pink and sunny yellow soon won out.

"Do you want to learn to sew?" Imogen asked after they'd selected one fabric for the bodice and three complementary ones for the skirt.

Ellery jumped up and down in excitement. "Let's measure and cut first, and then I'll teach you."

Imogen took Ellery's measurements and cut out the pieces they'd need. Since she'd been sewing since grade school herself, she wasn't worried about following a pattern. Imogen ran the curving lines of the bodice through the sewing machine. Then, when it came time to sew the skirt, she let Ellery sit with her and guide the material through, carefully keeping Ellery's small hands away from the moving needle.

"Excellent work," Imogen said when they finished the last seam. "Now, we attach the skirt to the bodice and start on the fun part."

"What's that?" Ellery's eyes were bright.

"Embellishment. You don't want a plain fairy costume, do you? We need wings and some bling." Since Ellery loved shiny, sparkly stuff, that wasn't a tough sell. "You look in that box for supplies while I take care of this." It only took a minute for Imogen to complete the sewing. Just long enough for Ellery to spread the contents of the remaining box all over the table. "Oh, my!" Imogen surveyed the cache.

Ellery was standing back with her hands on her hips, studying the table as if it held the wonders of the universe. "We need to organize."

"You are so right." Together, they moved like items into piles. Buttons, pieces of trim, spools of ribbon, feathers, yarn, sewing supplies, and costume jewelry.

"It's like a treasure chest," Ellery said when they were done, and Imogen had to agree.

"It's nice that these belonged to your great-grandmother," Imogen commented. "You're lucky to have things that were hers."

"They're not really mine." Ellery's tone was a little sorrowful. "I think Daddy owns it all."

"I think if you ask him, he'll give them to you," Imogen suggested. Patrick had given them space throughout the afternoon, which she appreciated.

"Can I ask now?" her eyes lit up.

"Go get him."

Ellery skipped out to the garage where Patrick was working and dragged him back into the dining room. First, she showed him the costume. Like a good dad, he oohed and aahed over it.

"But, Daddy, can't you see that it needs sparkle?"

"If you say so." He shot Imogen a look, asking for help.

"Ellery would like permission to use some of these items on her costume." Imogen waved her hand over the table.

"Fine with me," he said, focusing on the piles. He picked up an oversized, ornate red button. "I remember this. It was on my grandmother's good winter coat, the one she only wore to church." He was smiling, but Imogen watched his expression turn steely when he picked up a clumsily made bracelet.

"What's that?" Ellery asked. "I've never seen anything like that before."

"A charm bracelet," Patrick's voice was low. "I knew it was in the house somewhere, but…"

"Was it yours?" Imogen asked softly, trying to understand his reaction.

He shook his head. "I made it for my mother." His fingers closed in a fist around the bracelet.

"Ellery, will you run up to my bedroom and get the little basket on my dresser?" Imogen wanted a minute with Patrick without little ears nearby. "Are you all right?" she asked as soon as Ellery was out of the room.

Patrick relaxed his fist. "Yeah, just a reminder that Mom didn't take it with her when she left."

"What?" Imogen had understood that his mother died. "I thought she'd passed away." From what he'd said, both his parents had died, although he hadn't shared any details.

"She did," he answered, "not long after she abandoned us."

"I'm sorry," she whispered, sudden understanding coming to her. He'd been an abandoned child as well. That was doubtlessly adding to his desperation to make everything perfect for Ellery. "How old were you?"

"Eight, but she'd been… troubled long before that."

"You should keep that," Imogen said, gesturing to the charm bracelet, "or give it to Ellery when she's a little older. It'll mean something to her."

"You're right." He slipped the bracelet into his pocket. Unexpectedly, he reached for her and pulled her to him. He seemed to be seeking comfort, and she was happy to give him that. An idea struck her.

"How about a date night for us?" she asked, tilting her face up to his.

"I like it," Patrick responded, kissing her softly. "We could use some kid-free time."

He was definitely right about that. They needed to be a couple and not a parent and a caregiver, which seemed to be the roles they'd fallen into.

"Imogen," Ellery yelled from the top of the stairs.

"Yes?" she called. They'd debated about what Ellery should call her, finally deciding on her first name as the most appropriate and comfortable for everyone.

"Can I try a little of your perfume?" Ellery pleaded. "Just one squirt. Please."

Imogen laughed. "I should have known she couldn't resist my makeup tray. She's all girl," she said in a low voice to Patrick. "You are going to have such a time in the teenage years." She raised her voice a bit to respond to Ellery. "One squirt only."

"You've made her happy today," Patrick said, brushing another kiss across her lips. "I owe you."

"A date will go a long way toward paying that debt." She kept a smile on her face because she truly was happy at that moment, but the thought that she wouldn't be there to see Ellery grow into a teen and then a young woman saddened her.

16

Imogen walked into the bar to the sound of axes biting into wooden targets. After Patrick agreed to a night out, she'd asked him to pick the spot. Drinking beer and throwing axes seemed like a bad idea, especially when she spent her days teaching kids the correct way of walking while carrying safety scissors, but Patrick smiled, his eyes tracking to the back of the bar where the ax throwers clustered.

"Wild idea," she commented. "Alcohol and pointy objects."

"Perfect, if you ask me." He gave her a flirtatious grin and bumped his hip into her.

"Oh, go get us some beers," Imogen ordered with a shake of her head. He took her hand and she followed him to the bar, where he immediately cut through the crowd and caught the eye of the pretty bartender.

He held up two fingers, and a few seconds later, cold bottles slid across the bar to them. "Open a tab for me," he asked.

"Sure thing, darlin'," the bartender responded.

Imogen laughed when the woman walked away with a wiggle. "Is that the norm for you, or do you know her?"

"Never seen her before," he answered with a shrug.

"Do women always succumb to your charms so easily?" She could guess they did. It hadn't taken her long to.

He snaked his arm around her waist and guided her toward the ax-throwing area. Leaning his head closer to hers, he whispered, "Jealous?"

Imogen flipped her hand up so her wedding band caught the light. "I don't like women flirting with *my* husband."

He kissed her ear, taking a brief nibble on the lobe that sent a spike of desire through her. "You've got nothing to worry about, since you're the prettiest woman in the room. I'll be fending other guys off."

"I doubt that," she said. She was attractive, but so were several other women there who were dressed in a way meant to command men's attention. Besides, what guy would approach her with Patrick at her side? They would all recognize an alpha male when they saw one and steer clear. Not that she wanted anyone's attention but his.

"Ever done anything like this before?" he asked when they found an open lane and an attendant gave them axes and a two-minute safety lecture.

"Not even a little." She picked up the ax and hefted it in her hand. The wooden handle was smoothly polished and would slide easily from her grasp. "I don't know about this."

"It's awesome." He was clearly pumped about it. "It's like going to the shooting range to blow off steam."

"Do you do that?" she asked, wondering about how much was pent up inside his carefully controlled exterior.

"Sure." He was only half listening to her as he took aim. She waited until he'd thrown his ax. It hit just left of the bull's-eye. Not bad for a first throw.

"What drives you to the range?" His missions? His family? His ex? He had plenty of stressors in his life. She wondered again how he'd survived being abandoned as a kid. What scars were left from that?

"Huh?" He turned back to her and grabbed his beer, taking a swig.

"You know, what upsets you enough to make you want to shoot things?" She tried to keep her tone light, so he'd respond, but his eyes shuttered immediately. He wasn't going to talk about his feelings. She thought he'd turn away, but he swung back, his stance almost confrontational.

"Listen, wife of mine, I came here to drink some beer, throw some axes, and kiss my woman without a kid around." To prove his point, he hauled her to him and kissed her in a way that drew catcalls from the surrounding lanes. "Got that?" he asked when they drew apart. "This isn't a therapy session."

"Fine by me," she said, breaking free from him and stepping up to the line to make her throw. Two could play at this game. And it was good to be out of the house and free from parental responsibilities for the night. The entire night. Ellery was at a friend's house for a sleepover. She knew the friend's mom, who had been a room mom during the school year, so neither she nor Patrick had any reservations about Ellery's safety. She was probably having a blast. So why shouldn't Imogen?

She took aim, trying to block out the noise around her. She let the ax fly. It hit the board but too low.

"Nice try," he said with a smirk and jostled her as he took her spot at the line.

"I suppose you're going to show me how it's done?" she asked.

"Watch and learn, sweetheart." He let his ax fly, sending the tip into the top of the bull's-eye.

"Pretty good," she said of his awesome throw, "but I can do better." She was totally bluffing. No way could she beat him at this sort of skill, but she took careful aim. Her throw ended up on the board, nearer the center.

"Not bad." He grabbed her and yanked her back against him, kissing the side of her neck.

On his next and all following throws, he hit the bull's-eye. Each toss she made got a little closer, despite his best efforts to distract her with his touch, kiss, and the beers he bought. She stopped him from getting her another when she finished the third. He was ahead of her by a couple but seemed unfazed by it. His aim never slipped, even on his last throw when she grabbed his butt a second before he released the ax.

"No fair." He spun around to her, yanking her against him and kissing her. She responded to the kiss, forgetting they were in a crowded bar until his hand crept to her breast.

"I think it's time to go home," she said, batting his hand away. "I'll see about an Uber." She tapped the app open on her phone, thankful they'd used the service to get to the bar.

"One more toss each. To be the decision-maker." He handed her the ax.

"You know you won," she said. He'd outperformed her on every throw.

"That's not what we're playing for." His grin was wide and his eyes bright. He was definitely up to something. "We're playing for who gets to be on top tonight."

A surge of desire went through her. No matter who hit the bull's-eye, they would both be winners. She stepped up to the line and took aim. To her surprise, her ax sailed through the air and bit into the backstop dead in the center of the rings.

"Top that," she said, turning back to him.

"Not even going to try." He held his hands wide in mock defeat.

"Oh, no, you don't." She stopped him. "I'm not going to have it said that this was unfair. Take your shot."

He downed the rest of his beer and sauntered to the line, letting the ax go without so much as taking aim. It bounced off the backstop and dropped to the floor.

"See? You win." He closed the distance between them and whispered, "The living room floor?"

Imogen wasn't going to argue. She snatched her purse from the little table, grabbed his hand, and hauled him out of the bar. During the ride home, they carefully sat on either side of the car, not touching, only making small talk with the driver when he asked a question. She knew where her mind was, and she could guess Patrick was thinking the same sort of thoughts.

"Five minutes," Patrick said to her when they were home, his voice almost a growl. The sexual energy between them pulsed in the air. He checked the security system and did a quick check of the backyard, taking Mr. Bubblesworth out with him.

Imogen thought about changing into lingerie but decided her short skirt, tank top, and high-heeled sandals were just as good. She hit the playlist on her phone, finding a sultry tune that seemed just right. She was considering lighting some candles when he came back into the room. One look at him and she didn't care about romantic ambience. She just wanted him.

With her knee, she bumped the coffee table to the side, making a clear spot on the carpet at her feet.

"Is this good?" She reached for the hem of her top and pulled it over her head, tossing it aside.

"It's all good," he said and closed the distance between them. His hands circled her bare waist before sliding down over her butt. He pulled her against him so she could feel the hard ridge of his erection.

She gave him a thrust with her hips, enjoying the gasp that came from him. Not to be bested, he unclasped her lacy pink bra and yanked it off her. It sailed into a corner of the room. She pressed her nipples into his chest, rubbing them against the soft fabric of his shirt and moaning at the contact. His skin would feel even better, so she grabbed his shirt at the shoulders and pulled it over his head in one movement.

But that still wasn't enough. Her hands went to the button fly of his jeans. As she worked each one loose, she stroked her fingers up and down him. He bit his lip, and his head tipped back. She took that as an invitation to do what she wanted with him, so she dropped to her knees and worked his jeans over his hips and off. His boxers came next, until his dick was free and at mouth level for her.

His hands sank into her hair, massaging her scalp and pulling her closer to him. She didn't hesitate, but took him in, letting her tongue swirl around his tip and her teeth scrape along his hard length.

"Christ, woman," he muttered, and she felt his powerful body shudder. Emboldened, she sucked on him hard, tightening her lips around him. Her hands grasped his butt, squeezing the muscle and controlling the strokes. "I want to be inside you."

"You better have a condom in your wallet," she said, letting his dick go and slipping her hand into the pocket of his discarded jeans.

"Hell, yes, I do," he said, going to his knees in front of her. She found it quickly, and he took it from her. "First, you need to strip." His voice took on a commanding tone.

"What? I don't get any help from you?" she questioned as he stretched out on the floor, watching her. "Seems unfair, since I undressed you." She pretended to pout.

"I think you'll enjoy it as much as I will," he teased, his eyes focused on her breasts.

Maybe he deserved exactly what he asked for, she thought, rising to her feet. She sat for a moment on the edge of the sofa, where he could easily see up her skirt, and made a show of removing her sandals, stroking her fingers up her legs as she went. Standing again, she reached behind her to unzip her skirt and shimmied as she pushed it down, making sure her breasts swayed with each movement.

She had his rapt attention, and she loved it. Only her panties remained. They were pink lace to match the bra. She took her time pushing them down. When she stepped out of them, she dropped them on his chest. He snatched at them, clutching them in his hand.

"Come here," he growled.

"You don't want me to touch myself, too?" She didn't think she was that adventurous, but maybe…

His dark eyes went black with desire. "God, yes, but later."

"You're not ready," she said, with a nod to the condom, and laughed when he put it on in record time.

"Am now." He lifted his hips up as if to show her. "Ride me."

She didn't hesitate as she straddled him and dropped down onto him, taking him inside her in one thrust. She sucked in a breath. He was big, filling her, and it threatened the control she'd exerted over herself so far, but she held on. She squeezed around him and lifted her body before pounding back down. His hands came to her breasts, kneading and fondling as she continued to ride him. She'd never felt so powerful, so womanly, so alive. He matched her movements until it was a battle for control. She could no longer think of anything but him and this moment.

"Oh, Patrick," she whimpered, so close to flying apart. He reached between them, stroking a finger over her sensitive nub, and she could no longer keep herself together. The orgasm hit her, ripping through her in waves of ecstasy unlike anything she'd ever experienced. His hands gripped her hips, holding her in place as he pumped into her and found his release.

They stayed locked together until she collapsed next to him, pulling him to face her, and a contentment settled over her. He seemed to feel it, too, because all the tension went out of his face and body. She snuggled closer, relishing the sense of intimacy and the soft kisses he placed on her cheeks and brow.

She could get used to this. Her hands strayed down his back and rubbed over the scarred flesh there. She meant only to bring him comfort, but he stiffened, holding himself like a spring before release.

"Don't." His whisper was harsh, and he rolled away.

Cool air rushed over her, making her shiver despite the warm night. But it wasn't just the temperature of the room, it was his reluctance to let her in any more than he had. She'd gotten glimpses of the emotional scars he carried, but no more than that.

She felt tears come to her eyes. Before they could flow down her cheeks, she stood, gathering her clothes, and went up the stairs alone. An hour later, he crawled into bed next to her, but she felt as cut off from him emotionally as if he were on the other side of the world.

<h1 style="text-align:center">17</h1>

"Thank you. Yes, I appreciate your efforts," Imogen said into the phone before hanging up.

"What was that about?" Patrick asked, coming into the kitchen.

She hated to tell him. Since their date night—an outing she'd hoped would reduce his stress—he'd been more edgy than ever, more likely to snap at her or Ellery. Every instinct in Imogen wanted to soothe him emotionally the same way she'd wanted to touch his physical scars, but he wouldn't let her close enough to do either. He'd made that clear.

"The police," she admitted, knowing he wouldn't let it go. "They don't have any leads about the intruder or the calls I've received, so they've put it on the back burner."

"They're blowing it off?" Without waiting for her reply, he grabbed his phone from the counter and hit a button.

"Who are you calling?" Imogen asked.

"A buddy. He might be able to trace the numbers. Give me your phone." He held out his hand. She was tempted to walk away from him, since his attitude sucked. Reluctantly, she keyed in her pass code so he could see the log of calls.

Before she could say anything, he walked out the door. She watched him stalk around the yard while talking. With each step, he seemed to be putting more distance between them. She shook her head and focused on Ellery, who was watering the flowers in the window boxes attached to her playhouse.

Patrick made his way back toward the house, stopping for a minute to speak to Ellery. Imogen couldn't hear what he said to her, but it got a smile from the girl. At least things were better between Ellery and her father. Their relationship wasn't perfect, but Ellery seemed to be responding to Patrick's tenseness with concern and empathy, not the tantrums she might have had at one time.

"Any luck?" Imogen asked once Patrick returned to the house.

"Yeah, he'll look into the calls." He handed her phone back.

"And he'll be able to find out information the police couldn't?" She was doubtful, since the police had seemed to take her complaint seriously.

Patrick eyed her and hesitated as if weighing his words. "He has alternate methods."

"Legal ones, I hope." She didn't want anyone getting in trouble over her problems.

"Yes, but even if they weren't, I'd ask him to use them. I'm done with seeing you get harassed."

She shrugged. The calls had become almost an accepted part of her life. Sometimes she got overwhelmed by them. Unfortunately, Patrick had seen her at those moments. Most of the time she could ignore them. And they wouldn't last much longer. The trial was coming up soon, and then, hopefully, this nightmare would be over.

"It's a problem that has to get solved," he insisted. "You're sure you can't go to your handler?"

She let out an exasperated sigh. "We've been over this. I don't trust him. I don't want him to know any more than he already does."

"All right," Patrick agreed without an argument, and she was grateful that he seemed to accept it.

"I appreciate you trying to fix my problems, though." She wasn't lying about that. She just wished their situation weren't so complicated. "I know you've got a lot on your own plate."

"That's the truth," he muttered, turning to watch Ellery out the kitchen window. She'd moved to the picnic table where she had her Barbie doll and several outfits laid out. "I need to make sure Rachel never tries to claim her."

"Were you able to contact her?" Imogen knew that had been on his mind. Ellery's mother could cause him a host of problems, as Child Protective Services had warned. He needed Rachel to give up her legal rights, or he'd always be looking over his shoulder.

"I know where she is, but she won't respond to my calls. I guess abandoning her kid isn't enough, she has to be a pain in the ass, too."

Imogen wanted to wrap her arms around him, but she resisted. He wouldn't welcome the comfort she so desperately wanted to offer, not in that way. He was fine with sex and flirtation. He expected her to be a caregiver for Ellery, but other than that, she was pushed to a minor role in his life.

A squeal from outside made her focus her attention on Ellery. The Barbie doll she'd been dressing went flying into the grass, and, with one sweep of her arm, the outfits did too. Ellery stood, stomping her feet and holding her arms stiffly at her sides.

Patrick rushed out the door. "What is it? What's wrong?"

"The stupid dress won't go on the stupid doll," Ellery screamed, her face red with anger.

Imogen followed Patrick outside, feeling a pang of guilt. The dress was a tight fit, and it was difficult getting the long sleeves over the doll's rigid arms.

"The doll can wear a different dress." Patrick picked one up from the grass. "What about this one?"

"She's going out with Ken to a fancy place. She can't wear a sundress," Ellery screeched.

Imogen assessed the situation. Should she interfere or let Patrick work it out? He had wanted her help with Ellery, so she supposed she could step in. And one of her goals for the summer was for Ellery to be more resilient. This could be a good learning opportunity for that.

"Ellery," Imogen said in a calm tone, "please pick up your doll and her clothes and put them back on the picnic table."

"I won't." Ellery crossed her arms in front of her, reminding Imogen of how she'd behaved when she first went to foster care. They'd made strides since then, but this was a definite slide backward, which meant it had to be handled carefully.

"Would you want to be tossed aside when the problem wasn't your fault?" Imogen asked and got a glare from Patrick. Shoot, that's exactly what had happened to Ellery. Fortunately, the girl didn't seem to make the connection as she toed her doll.

"I'll help." Patrick gathered up the scattered items before Ellery could even move.

Imogen sighed. That wasn't teaching Ellery the right thing to do.

"Dress her," Ellery ordered, handing her father the half-dressed doll.

"Sure, honey. We'll just… uh…" He tried to work the dress over the doll's head, but it got stuck on the arms. He took it off and repeated the action, with the same results.

"See, you made it wrong." Ellery shot the accusation at Imogen.

"Remember, I showed you how to put that dress on her," Imogen said, not reacting to the angry tone. "Do you need to see again?"

"No," Ellery snapped. "Daddy'll do it."

Imogen expected Patrick to correct his daughter's words, but he didn't. He kept his head down over the doll, so Imogen walked away, retreating back into the house. She picked up a mystery novel she was reading and went to the front porch, where she settled into a rocker and tried to read, but she was too upset.

Was it Ellery's treatment of her or Patrick's that was harder to bear? She didn't know. Both hurt, especially since she'd been making strides with the girl, or so she had felt. The man, though. She wasn't getting any closer to him, not in an emotional sense. But what had she expected from their arrangement?

She puffed out a breath and opened her book. Her eyes skimmed unseeingly over the lines until she heard the door open behind her.

"Imogen," Patrick said, "can you show me how to do this?"

She glanced at him. He held the doll and the dress in his hands. Wordlessly, she took both and demonstrated how to negotiate the arms into the sleeves and snap the back.

"Thanks. I'll…" He hesitated. Was he going to apologize?

"You'll what?" she asked, hoping for a minute of understanding.

"I'll show Ellery so she can do it herself next time."

Imogen wanted to remind him that that's exactly what she had suggested in the backyard, but she held her tongue on that subject. "You can't always fix things for her. That doesn't help her. De-escalate by being calm and talking her through the situation."

"That might work for you, but…"

"It needs to work for you, too. I'm not always going to be here." Imogen didn't like saying it, but it was true.

His face hardened. "That's right. You're not. Besides, Ellery's problems are my fault, and I need to bear the burden of them."

His words couldn't have hurt more if he'd slapped her. "Then what's my role here?" she asked softly. "Wasn't I supposed to help with her behavioral issues? Teach her to mitigate them herself?"

"Yeah, but I need a permanent solution." He scrubbed a hand over his face and stared out over the front yard. "That is, if I'm going to keep being a SEAL."

She looked at him in surprise, but he was already walking out of the house. This was the first time he'd mentioned possibly not returning to the service. No wonder he was stressed, if that was on his mind along with everything else.

But recognizing that didn't lessen the hollow feeling inside her.

18
____

"Make sure you stay in the house and leave the security system on," Patrick said to Imogen a few days later. He was standing at the door, waiting for Ellery to come down.

"You've told me that three times." Imogen's smile was tolerant. "I've got it."

He didn't like leaving her alone and unprotected, but he had plans for the day. He had to drop Ellery off for a day of observation and therapy at Child Protective Services and then meet his ex. Rachel had finally responded to his phone calls, but she wasn't being particularly cooperative. If he wanted to see her, he had a short time frame, since she was leaving for a luxury honeymoon with her new man in three days.

At least she had implied that she'd gladly sign the papers Patrick's attorney had drawn up, and relinquish her parental rights to Ellery. He was clinging to that silver lining. Because other than that, he was floundering. He needed to make a career decision, but more than that, he needed to manage his relationships with Imogen and Ellery better. He knew he'd hurt Imogen lately, that she was only trying to help. But he saw all this as his mess and his responsibility. He should never have drawn Imogen into it, and he might not have if she hadn't been in danger.

And Ellery was picking up on the tension he couldn't fully hide. She was still sweet and loving some of the time, but then her mood would shift, seemingly for no reason, and she'd get angry or burst into tears. Imogen kept trying to teach him how to handle those situations, and he thought he was learning, but it was slow going—and he wasn't used to that. His career had been built on tackling problems head-on, overcoming them, and moving forward. Going around in circles like this made him feel like a caged animal.

"Good luck with Rachel today," Imogen said. She'd put up with his difficult attitude, meeting his sharp edges with softness, which only made him feel like more of an ass.

"I appreciate that," he said as Ellery came down the stairs, her footsteps dragging. She didn't want to go. She'd made that clear. "Ready, honey?"

"I guess. Bye, Imogen. Can you make spaghetti for dinner? With garlic bread?" the little girl pleaded.

"I think I can manage that. I'll see you guys tonight." Imogen walked to the door with them. Patrick paused on the other side, waiting for the click of the lock and the beep of the security system. When he heard those, he felt marginally better, but those safety measures were no replacement for him being there. Oh well. He'd done everything he could, including asking the police to patrol the street more frequently than usual. Given the break-in, they'd agreed.

After a silent ride, he pulled into the parking lot of the county building where CPS's office was located. He intended to check Ellery in, make sure she got to her first appointment, and take off to see Rachel. If all went well, he'd be back in plenty of time to pick Ellery up. He'd laid out the plan carefully in his head, including time estimates. It would work.

"I don't wanna go," Ellery said when he shut the engine off.

They'd been over this before. "We don't get a choice, kiddo."

"You could stay with me, couldn't you?" Ellery's voice was uncharacteristically small.

"I've got to be somewhere today," he said, though his heart broke for his girl. He had to deal with Rachel, since she'd only given him this short window of opportunity, but he didn't want to tell Ellery exactly what was going on.

"You sure?" Ellery asked.

He started to nod, but then he stopped himself, seeing the situation from a different angle. No, he wasn't sure. Why should he have to abandon his daughter again, on a day when she clearly needed him, to chase down his irresponsible ex? Damn Rachel and her antics. He wasn't going to let her steal any more time with Ellery from him.

"You know what? I can change my plans. I want to spend the day with you instead." Ellery's expression transformed in an instant, hope beaming from her eyes. "Let's go." He got out of the truck and took her hand as they walked toward the building.

Patrick had no idea what to expect from the day. If he had, he might have sought out Rachel as the easier option, because every moment was a reminder of the damage she, and he, had caused their daughter. Between the two of them, they'd messed Ellery up. He had few regrets in life, but this one was enormous, he thought, as he stood behind a one-way mirror and watched Ellery interact with other kids.

One minute she was sweet, joyous, and creative, but the next her trust issues were evident in how she reacted to other kids and the therapist who was in the room with them. It was tough to see, but no less than he deserved.

"She seems better," Anita, the lead CPS representative on their case, said from her position next to him.

"Does she?" he asked.

"I think so. She seems more willing to engage with the other kids, but we'll see what the therapist has to say about it."

He continued to watch as the other children left and the therapist stayed to work with Ellery one-on-one. It wasn't what he expected. The therapist didn't ask Ellery questions. Instead, the two of them played in different ways. First a kids' board game, followed by drawing and coloring and then time with dolls. None of it seemed like the therapy sessions he imagined, and it was certainly nothing like the debriefing sessions after his missions.

Children had to be handled differently. He knew that, intellectually, but it was a lesson he had difficulty putting into practice. Imogen helped with that. She got Ellery. He felt bad about his behavior toward Imogen lately. He could promise her protection, but other than that, he didn't seem to be giving her what she needed.

"The therapist is ready to talk with you," Anita said and led him to the same conference room they'd been in before.

The team around the table was smaller and looked more sympathetic than the group he'd faced when he first petitioned for custody, but he felt alone. The previous time, he'd had his lawyer with him... and Imogen had been there, an ally of sorts, even if he barely knew her then. Today it was just him facing up to his own shortcomings.

"Hello, Captain Nelson. I'm Dr. Aimee Johnson," the therapist said, offering her hand for him to shake. "Although we haven't met before, this is my third observation with Ellery." She went on to list the other dates for him. One was when Ellery entered foster care and the other just before the first custody hearing. "How have you been managing at home?"

"Fine," he said.

Dr. Johnson smiled. "I don't think that's quite true. We're on your side, you know." The tilt of her head indicated Anita and the other social worker. "It's okay to be honest if you're struggling."

He took a breath. "I wouldn't say struggling, but there have been difficult moments." He told them about the recent scene with the Barbie doll and some other moments when Ellery's behavior had gone off the rails.

"And what are you doing about these episodes?"

"Trying to be patient," he said, "and de-escalate." He used Imogen's word, because he realized that she was right.

"That's good," Dr. Johnson said. "It's a start. Our goal is for Ellery's behavior to normalize and be typical of any child her age."

"How close are we to that?" he asked, even though he could guess the answer.

"It's going to take time, a stable, loving environment, and the right responses from you."

In other words, they were a hell of a long way from where they needed to be. He felt the clock ticking. If he stayed in the SEALs, his next mission was less than five months away. Was that enough time? Or would leaving then set Ellery back? He wanted to ask, but he was pretty damn sure he didn't want to hear the answer.

Any happiness he'd felt earlier in the day when Ellery begged him to stay with her disappeared. All he could see was the hard work ahead, but giving Ellery a better life was worth any effort on his part. He didn't know where to begin, so he listened to Dr. Johnson's report, filing the information away in his head as if it were a briefing prior to a deployment. It was good intel, but it didn't tell him what to do in the here and now.

"What do I do?" he asked when the doctor finished speaking. "How do I fix her? Can you give me concrete suggestions?"

"We can, and we will," the therapist replied, "though it's not a question of 'fixing' Ellery so much as responding to her in ways that will enable her to learn and internalize healthier reactions to her emotions and surroundings. We can offer you options on how to handle certain behaviors when they manifest, and that's our plan for the next hour. But—with the utmost respect—I suggest that you also do some work on yourself in this process."

"What do you mean?" He felt himself tense. In his experience, "with respect" was a polite way of calling someone a jackass. What was she implying?

"I sense some pent-up anxiety on your part," she said gently, "and your background check revealed that your mother left when you were young. You and Ellery may share some issues, and it would be good for both of you to deal with those." She looked him in the eye. "I realize that this may feel like a personal attack, and I assure you that's not my intention. You clearly have succeeded admirably in your career, and you're making good progress in building a healthy relationship with your daughter. But in order to help Ellery most effectively, it's important for you to understand what may drive some of your own responses to situations—so you can help and guide her."

He gripped the armrests, trying to control his anger. This meeting was supposed to be about Ellery, not him. But he forced himself to breathe normally and evaluate Dr. Johnson's words as if they were more of that pre-deployment intel. He couldn't deny that his mother's actions had affected him as a child—and, more importantly, he'd do anything and everything he could to avoid hurting Ellery the same way. After another moment to settle his emotions, he gave Dr. Johnson a small nod and asked if she could recommend a private therapist he and Ellery could see together.

An hour later, he left the room armed with advice and a booklet about dealing with traumatized children. The word trauma meant something different to him, but he was learning the CPS lingo and making adjustments. Imogen would understand all this, but he couldn't rely on her forever. He had to become Ellery's primary caregiver and guide in life. The responsibility was staggering, but he wasn't backing down from the challenge.

"Can we get ice cream on the way home?" Ellery asked when she skipped toward him in the hall outside the conference room. "We can take a milkshake home for Imogen."

"That's a great idea. What flavor do you think she'd want?" he asked, taking Ellery's hand and heading for the door.

"Strawberry," Ellery said. "That's what she always gets."

"She does?" He hadn't noticed, but he wasn't surprised that Ellery had. She was a perceptive kid.

"Of course, silly." Ellery beamed up at him, and his heart warmed in his chest.

Oh, yeah. Whatever it took to make her happy and healthy, he'd do.

19

Breathe. Breathe. Breathe.

Imogen slowly pulled air into her lungs and let it out, fighting against a panic that went bone deep. She was trapped, locked in the trunk of a moving car, being driven God knew where.

Somewhat calmer, she felt above her in the cramped space, seeking a lever or pull cord. Fortunately, her captors had tied her hands in front of her rather than behind her back. Her ankles were bound as well, limiting her movement.

Come on, she thought in frustration. Didn't all cars have a trunk release on the inside? Wasn't there some kind of law that required it? She remembered reading that somewhere, so she started her search again, rolling over in the tight, dark space to feel along the edge of the trunk.

She'd searched here already, but maybe she'd missed it. Rough-textured carpet, metal, something sticky, but nothing that felt like a release.

Fresh tears came to her eyes, but she squeezed them back. Crying wouldn't help. Neither would regrets, and she'd had plenty of those in the minutes since her kidnapping. She should have stayed in the house as Patrick had told her to do. But Mr. Bubblesworth had been dying for a walk. His constant trips between the leash and the front door said that as loudly as any words could have. Finally, she'd given in. It was a beautiful summer day, after all, and she wanted to go outside almost as much as the puppy did.

She'd just made it to the road when a car pulled up, blocking her path. Two men jumped out and grabbed her, yanking Mr. Bubblesworth away despite his attempts to protect her. She'd struggled, but one of them—tall and strong—had picked her up and tossed her in the trunk, then the car had sped off. After a few minutes the car had stopped and the men reopened the trunk. She'd tried to spring out and run, but they were too fast. One pinned her inside the trunk, the other tied her hands and feet, and then they slammed the lid again. She'd caught a glimpse of trees overhead, but that was it.

The car took a sudden hard left, and she winced when her head smacked against the trunk wall. Dammit. She rolled onto her back, staring upward in the darkness. Where were they taking her? She'd kept that question at bay, but she couldn't any longer. Other questions came hard on its heels. What would they do to her? Who were they?

When would she learn not to trust anyone?

Tears flowed from her eyes, running off the sides of her face. She'd trusted Grant. She'd even thought she'd loved him, and look where that had gotten her. She'd trusted her handler, at least at first, and she'd endured months of vile phone calls and harassment.

She'd trusted Patrick to keep her safe. And he probably would have if she'd stayed in the house as he asked. That's what her rational brain told her. She stifled a sob. When she'd needed Patrick's protection most, he hadn't been there for her. Oh, it wasn't his fault, she knew, but she couldn't help the resentment that rose in her. Or maybe that resentment was for the role he'd confined her to in his life.

None of those thoughts helped. She had to think. She shoved away her questions and worry to focus on her situation. The kidnapping had happened right in front of the house, which meant that the security cameras might have picked it up. That was a hopeful thought. She could trust Patrick to check the recording when he realized she was missing, but when would that be? She had no idea when he was supposed to get home. It had been midafternoon when she set out with Mr. Bubblesworth, but Patrick could be away for several more hours. She groaned, any hope she felt evaporating.

Okay, so she couldn't rely on him to rescue her. She had to do this herself. Since there was no trunk release that she could find, she'd have to wait for her opportunity when her kidnappers opened the lid. She tried to stretch her tight muscles. She'd have to act quickly and decisively, and she could pass the time by mentally preparing herself for that… because it was the only way she was going to get free.

That would keep her focused and the fear at bay.

Ellery slurped her milkshake loudly. They'd made a stop at the Dairy Dock and gotten treats, just as Ellery had asked. By the time Patrick pulled onto his street, he was feeling pretty good about life. His daughter was… better… and he was feeling more confident about being a dad.

When he saw Mr. B sitting on the front porch, his leash attached to his collar, all happiness dropped away. What the hell was going on?

"Stay here," he said to Ellery. "You can turn the radio up." He left the truck running but locked the doors as he got out. If he'd been carrying a gun, he'd have drawn it. Something was wrong, every one of his instincts screamed.

"What's going on, Mr. B?" Patrick rested his hand on the dog's head. "Where is she?" As if trying to answer, the dog whined and slumped to the floor.

Patrick tried the door, finding it locked. That might be a positive, but it didn't explain why Mr. B was outside by himself. Patrick unlocked the door, checking the security pad as soon as he entered. It was armed. He keyed in his code.

"Imogen?" he called, his eyes sweeping the living room. He moved next to the dining room and kitchen before searching the upstairs. Nothing. She was gone.

He played possible scenarios in his head. Her car was parked in the driveway, so she hadn't driven anywhere. No one had forcibly entered the house. But the dog outside, leash attached, suggested she was headed out for a walk when something or someone stopped her.

He retraced his steps to the living room where he'd left his laptop, taking a second to peek out the window at Ellery in the truck. He could see her drinking her milkshake and singing along to the radio. She was fine for the moment.

He booted up his computer and went to the security system's online site, entering his password and code. From there, he could access the exterior cameras that were triggered by movement. In less than two minutes, he found the scene that made his blood run cold. As Imogen stepped off the porch with Mr. B, a car angled to a stop in front of the house. Two guys, wearing baseball caps pulled low, charged at her. She didn't have time to react before they pulled Mr. B away and were on her.

Patrick watched as they shoved her into the car's trunk and slammed it closed. Then they were headed down the street. The entire episode took less than fifteen seconds, according to the timer on the camera.

"Son of a bitch," Patrick swore as he replayed the footage. He needed something to go on. The car was a silver sedan. Too many of those on the road. He slowed the playback, squinting at the screen. As the car pulled away, the rear license plate became visible for a nanosecond. He froze the frame and grabbed his phone.

Even though he'd been let down by the police department's response to the threats and the intruder, they'd take kidnapping seriously. Patrick would bet on that. He called 9-1-1, then made a quick call to the mom of one of Ellery's friends. He wanted to join the hunt for Imogen, but he couldn't do that while Ellery was with him.

Ellery was still happily entertaining herself when he got back outside. "Change of plans, honey," he told her. "You've got a playdate with Sarah." He feared that news might trigger a meltdown, but thankfully she took it in stride. He threw the truck in gear and drove the short distance to Sarah's house, dropped Ellery off with quick thanks to Sarah's mother and a promise to explain later, and headed for the police station.

They might not welcome his interference, but they were going to have to live with that, because he had to be doing something to help get Imogen back. Otherwise, he'd dwell on his own guilt. He'd worried that the guys harassing her would get more daring as the court date approached, but he hadn't thought...

He should have, he realized, but his attention had been too fragmented between Ellery and his other worries. He should have thought through the possibilities, the threats, and prioritized Imogen's protection. Hadn't that been his deal with her? God, he'd failed her.

He wouldn't fail to find her. Beating the clock was all that mattered now. The sooner she was rescued the better. The longer they had her, the greater the danger. He had that thought in mind when he pulled up in front of the police station and jumped out. The sergeant at the desk directed him to where an officer was hanging up the phone.

"You Patrick Nelson?" the man asked, giving him a rapid appraisal.

"That's me," Patrick said, not taking time for pleasantries. "Have you found my wife?"

"We just had a report from the desk clerk at a motel on Route 3. He saw a vehicle that matched the one you reported. Two men pulled a woman from the trunk. The clerk said she came out fighting, but they overpowered her and took her into a room."

"Let's go." What the hell were they waiting for?

"It's probably not going to be that simple." The officer held up his hands. "I understand you're upset, but I'm going to ask you to stay here or, better yet, go home and let us handle this."

"Like hell I will," Patrick said, facing the other man down. A brass tag on his uniform read Anders. "Listen, Officer Anders, if your wife was kidnapped and put in the trunk of a car, would you go home and wait quietly for news?"

"Not a chance," the officer admitted. He gave a short sigh. "I can't stop you from following me, but don't get involved."

Patrick got back in his truck and kept behind the unmarked police car until it pulled into the lot of the motel. He peeled off then, parking well away from the silver sedan. He didn't like the idea of staying in his truck, but he knew the risks of interfering in an organized operation, so he forced himself to wait and watch as the police knocked on the door of a unit before hitting it with a battering ram.

At that point, Patrick couldn't keep still. He jumped out and ran closer. He could hear a scuffle inside the room and the sound of breaking glass, but no shots. When the two men he'd seen on the security video came out in handcuffs, Patrick barreled into the room.

Imogen sat on the edge of the bed. A police officer was cutting the rope that bound her wrists and ankles. She looked up at him, her eyes meeting his, and then the police started peppering her with questions.

"Can you give her a minute?" Patrick demanded, not liking the paleness of her skin, the tight lines around her mouth.

"I'm all right," she said, lifting her chin. "Ask me what you have to, officer."

"Sir, you need to wait outside," a state police officer said to him.

Reluctantly, Patrick went out the door and leaned against the building. He'd wanted to rush to her and take her in his arms, but nothing about her body language or expression had been welcoming. Did she blame him for this? Probably, and he deserved that. She appeared to be unharmed, but he'd still failed her.

Almost an hour passed before she came out and headed for Anders's car.

"Imogen?" Patrick said. She paused but then, without looking at him, got in the police vehicle and was driven away.

20

Imogen nervously buttoned and unbuttoned the borrowed navy-blue blazer she wore. She was exhausted, but she'd made it. Court would be in session any minute. She would testify, and hopefully then her life could go back to normal. She had no idea what normal looked like anymore, but the trial brought her one step closer to working that out.

After being rescued by the police, she'd been transferred to a safe house to await the court date, which had only been a week away. She'd spent the time being grilled by the district attorney's office about the threats on her life. Thankfully, they were taking the situation seriously and investigating the source of the calls and notes. Imogen had no doubt the source would connect back to Grant's father.

That was one thing in her life she was confident about. Everything else was… complicated. It had been a lonely week without Patrick and Ellery. The DA had offered to place a guard at Patrick's house and allow her to return there, but she'd opted for the safe house because she didn't know what her relationship with Patrick was at this point.

He'd been there as her captors were being hauled away, but he'd looked so angry when he stormed into the motel room. She saw his expression in her head again. Maybe it hadn't been anger, but concern. She wasn't sure, but either way, she had to make a break from him. She didn't need him to protect her now, and he'd made it clear that he didn't want her interfering in how he raised Ellery.

She was locked out, and that hurt… but their relationship had never been intended to be anything but temporary. She knew she'd have to see him again. Her belongings, even her dog, were at his house, but all that would have to wait until the trial was over. She couldn't handle both issues at the same time.

"All rise," the bailiff called, announcing that court was now in session.

She stood at her seat behind the prosecutor's table, clutching the rail in front of her. Being here felt surreal. She'd waited for this event for over a year, and it was finally happening.

"Be seated," the bailiff commanded once the judge had seated himself at the bench.

As Imogen resettled herself, she glanced to the side and caught her ex-boyfriend's eye. Grant was across the aisle, behind his father, who wore a finely tailored suit and looked as though the trial were an inconvenience. But it wasn't Grant's father who held her attention. It was Grant. The hatred in his gaze made her shiver and look away. That wasn't how she remembered him. She closed her eyes and tipped her head down, recalling their last conversation when he'd pleaded with her to withdraw her accusations. Despite his anger when she'd refused, she hadn't seen the hatred in him that was evident now. Had she been blind to his real nature?

As opening statements began, she could feel Grant's eyes on her, feel the heat of his glare. How had she thought he was someone she could spend her life with? She'd once trusted him with her heart and even thought she might want to marry him. How wrong she'd been.

She fought the image, but Patrick's face came to her mind. Their relationship had been temporary, nothing but a convenience for both of them, and yet… he was the one her heart yearned for. Was she just foolish when it came to love? Did she put her faith and heart into impossible relationships?

She couldn't think about that now. She had to focus on the court proceedings. Tuning in, she listened to the defense attorney's opening statement, in which he claimed that Grant's father's connection to the victim was circumstantial and the DA had no proof of his involvement in anything illegal.

Imogen wanted to scoff, but she schooled her expression and stared straight ahead. Throughout the morning, evidence was presented and witnesses called. When the lunch recess came, she slipped quickly from the courtroom, fearful of facing Grant and his deadly stare. A confrontation with him was the last thing she needed.

The prosecutor caught her outside the courtroom. "You ready?"

"I think so," Imogen said, "but I'm nervous."

"You shouldn't be. You've got the truth on your side." A courier approached and handed the attorney a sealed envelope. "Excuse me, Ms. Mendel." He walked away to a quiet corner, and she saw him slit the envelope open and give a satisfied nod.

In the afternoon, the trial continued, and Imogen longed for it to be like the terse and pithy legal battles that took place on television shows. Those episodes featured the few interesting parts and skipped over the plodding moments where the opposing sides formulated their cases. Finally, it was her turn to testify.

"Do you swear to tell the whole truth…" The bailiff spoke the words in a monotone.

"I do," she answered and sat in the witness stand.

The questions from the district attorney were just what she'd been told to expect, designed to draw out what she had seen at the construction office that night and the story of how she'd reported the information. She noticed several jury members nodding along as if believing every word she'd said.

"And during the past year, Ms. Mendel, have you been living in witness protection, forced to move to a new town and change jobs because of what you witnessed?"

"That's correct," she confirmed.

"And is it also true that for several months you have been receiving harassing phone calls and threats against your person and well-being?"

"It is," she said. She hadn't expected this to come up during her testimony.

"Your Honor, the state brings additional felony charges against the defendant for criminal threatening connected to this case."

"Objection," the defense attorney declared. "This is the first my client or I have heard of this."

"I've just received confirmation from my office that the threats to Ms. Mendel can be traced to the defendant and the defendant's son," the DA said.

"You bitch," Grant snarled, standing suddenly. The judge banged his gavel, but Grant kept going, raising his voice to be heard over the commotion. "You didn't have the sense to keep your goddamn mouth shut."

"You…" Imogen stood on shaky legs. He was behind the phone calls and emails? And the kidnapping—was Grant implying he'd arranged that, too? The men who'd been arrested had either not known who hired them or refused to say. But it seemed implausible that it was unrelated to all the other harassment.

"Shut up, Grant," his father barked.

She shifted her gaze to the prosecutor, who didn't seem surprised by Grant's outburst. He signaled to a bailiff, who closed in on Grant and slapped handcuffs on him when he refused to accompany him quietly. He continued to spew hatred at her as he was led from the courtroom.

Imogen wanted to run and hide to avoid hearing his tirade, but she couldn't. Her feet were rooted to the spot. She'd once loved Grant, and he was… he was a monster. He'd robbed her of peace of mind for a year.

"In light of the new charges, Your Honor," the defense attorney said, "I'd like to request a continuance."

"I would imagine you would." The judge slapped his gavel down. "This case will reconvene one week from today."

"It's not over?" She could barely speak above a whisper when the prosecutor approached her. "I'll have to testify more?"

"Let's see what happens when the defense attorney reviews the new charges and evidence. My office thinks the case may go in a very different direction. My assistant will drive you back to the safe house, and I'll call you with updates."

Imogen let herself be led away, and in fifteen minutes she was back in the small room that had been hers for the past week. She still felt numb as she checked her phone for messages.

They want to bargain, a message from the DA's office read. Was that a good sign? Her legal knowledge was limited, but she thought that usually meant no trial would occur. Dare she let herself hope?

Over the next hours, she paced her room, her phone clutched in her hand until it finally rang.

"Good news," the prosecutor informed her. "You won't have to testify again."

"Will he go to prison?" Imogen asked, not letting herself feel relief until she was certain.

"Yes. I can't give you all the details yet, but you don't need to worry anymore."

"What about Grant, his son?" If Grant went free or if she had to testify against him in court… she wasn't sure she had the strength to do that.

"A similar situation. The charges against him are severe," the prosecutor assured her. "You can relax. It's over."

She thanked the prosecutor, left the safe house, and crossed the street to a little park, where she sat on a bench. Slowly, she let the truth sink in. *It was truly over*. The harassment—*Grant's* harassment—was all over. She could go back to her old life. Or could she?

Her life before all this had been wrapped up with Grant's. She didn't see how she could go back to that town and the people she'd known as his girlfriend… but her life in Hartsville wasn't really hers either. She liked the school where she'd taught and the sense of community, but her life there had been a fake one created by witness protection, to which she'd added a sham marriage.

She couldn't think of Patrick, not now. He was part of this interlude in her life that she had to move on from. Where would she go now? The world was suddenly open to her, but the freedom it offered held no appeal. The sunny house at the end of the lane near the woods did, but it was no longer hers. Patrick and Ellery were becoming their own family. As they should, she knew… but where did that leave her?

153

21

———————

Patrick walked through the small airport in Key West, Florida, and caught an Uber to the famed southernmost city in the country. If Rachel had agreed to meet him at the airport, he'd have made the next flight out of here and gotten home to Ellery hours sooner. But Rachel didn't give a damn for his convenience or Ellery's happiness.

Rachel had even had the audacity to be pissed about taking time to meet at all, since she was still on an extended honeymoon. It was clear she couldn't be bothered with her daughter, not even to relinquish custody. But it was all par for the course with her. All Patrick needed was her signature on two documents, and any connection to her would be broken forever.

Cause for celebration, in his mind, but his joy was dimmed by what happened between him and Imogen. He'd heard the court case was over. The news had reported the entire story of how her ex-boyfriend had verbally attacked her in court and how he and his father had ended up cutting plea deals. In the week prior to the trial, investigators had spoken with him about his knowledge of the threats against her. He'd been happy to tell them how Imogen had lived in fear, suspecting her handler of selling her out and being powerless to change the situation. He hoped they all rotted in prison over it.

Patrick had sent texts to Imogen after the trial was over, but they'd gone unanswered. In the messages, he'd asked how she was and if she needed anything. She hadn't responded to any of his attempts to reach her. He shouldn't be surprised. Ellery asked about her every day, and as much as Patrick wanted to comfort the girl, he'd been honest and said he didn't know if they would see Imogen again. His daughter's tears had nearly broken his heart, and the fact that he was powerless to solve the problem only added to his frustration.

Even the cheerful vibe of Duval Street didn't temper Patrick's mood. Neither did the sight of the luxury resort on the ocean. Rachel had always wanted to snag herself a rich guy, and it seemed she had succeeded. Patrick headed into the lobby where Rachel had promised to meet him and was unsurprised not to find her there. Investigating a cabana area near the pools, he spotted her lazing in the sun with a big floppy hat on her head and a tropical drink in her hand.

"Hello, Rachel," he said. "You were supposed to meet me."

She shrugged. "You found me. Drink?"

"No, thanks." He looked at her and wondered how he had ever cared for her. They'd never been in love, but they had been friends and lovers. That should mean something, but it didn't.

"Sit," she said. "You're blocking my sun."

"I just need you to sign these papers, and I'll get out of the damn state." He pulled them from the folder he carried.

She huffed and swung her legs to the ground, holding out her hand for the documents. "I don't see why you had to track me down on my honeymoon for this."

The polite thing to do would be to ask about her husband, but Patrick saw no reason for the niceties. "I wanted to get this over with and get on with my life. I'd think you'd want that, too."

"I suppose." She flipped through the pages, seeming to read sections here and there. "Lawyer-speak. What the hell does this all say?"

"It's pretty simple. Sign on the line and you relinquish all rights to Ellery."

"All? What if I want to see her someday?"

Patrick had to suppress his desire to knock the silly hat off her head and force a pen into her hand. She was toying with him. He knew it, but it still sent him into a fury. "If you wanted her, you shouldn't have abandoned her last March."

"I left her with the nanny," Rachel said.

"Who had no contact information for you and no money to support Ellery on. You gave her no choice but to turn Ellery over to foster care, and you knew that." Patrick made her failings clear.

Rachel's lips formed into a pout. "You don't have to get nasty about it. I'm not the worst mother in the world."

"That's debatable," he said.

"You're one to talk. Where were you for the first six years of Ellery's life? Huh? On the other side of the world, that's where." Her voice had risen, attracting the attention of nearby sunbathers.

"You're right, and I'm not arguing that. I was serving my country and paying you child support with the understanding that you were caring for our daughter. Imagine my surprise to find that you hadn't been."

Rachel turned her face away from him in a visual snub, and he had to walk away from her.

"I'm going to call my brother and check in on Ellery," Patrick said. "She's doing well, by the way. I thought I'd mention that, since you didn't ask." He strode off, going past pools and palm trees until he stood on the edge of the ocean.

Taking out his phone, he hit the button to dial Todd.

"Hey, bro," Todd answered. "How's it going?"

"It sucks," Patrick said. "How's Ellery?"

"She's fine. Do you want to say hi to Daddy?" Todd called.

"Hi, Daddy." Ellery's high-pitched voice made Patrick smile despite his anger at Rachel.

"Now you go on outside," Todd said to Ellery, "and we'll pretend like we weren't having a squirt gun fight in the kitchen."

Over the phone, Patrick could hear Ellery's giggles and the slam of the back door.

"What did Rachel do to piss you off?" Todd asked.

"Didn't ask about Ellery," Patrick said. He'd taken a picture of Ellery right before leaving home in case Rachel asked to see one. "And she doesn't seem the least bit regretful about abandoning her." That was even worse. "What the hell is wrong with her?" He knew his brother couldn't answer the question, but he had to say it.

"Nothing you can fix," Todd declared. "You've got to remember that. Now, get the papers signed and come home."

"Why? Is something wrong there?" He'd heard Ellery. She seemed fine. Was it Imogen? Was she okay? The lack of contact with her was killing him.

"Nothing's wrong, but I know you," his brother said. "You want to take on Rachel's problems—and she's got a shitload of them—and make everything better. News flash: Rachel is who she is, and you can't fix that, even if you think she's wrong or unhappy or misguided. I think she's evil, and Ellery is better off without a mother like that." There was a pause. "I'm just saying that you'll never make her care, bro, so stop trying."

"Fine. I should make the flight this evening. I'll be home late. Take care." Patrick hung up and looked at the water before him. The ocean was beautiful in the afternoon sunshine, but he barely processed it. What had Todd meant about him trying to fix other people's problems? Was that how his brother saw him?

He was going to ask that question when he got home, but first… Rachel. He strode back toward the cabana, vowing to himself to get the job done and leave.

Patrick was tired when he pulled into his driveway at midnight. Flying to Florida and back and fighting with his ex had drained him, but he'd gotten what he wanted. Once Rachel got bored with trying to bait him, she'd signed away all rights to Ellery forever.

Patrick felt bad for his little girl and knew down the road he'd face questions from her about Rachel, but he'd deal with that when the time came. For now, he had something to follow up on with his brother.

"Awesome, you're back." Todd got off the sofa and muted the television when Patrick walked in the door. "It's late. Mind if I crash here for the night?"

"Nope. Happy to have you," he said. "How's Ellery?"

"She's great. She went to bed without a peep." Todd grinned. "Well, after she convinced me to take her out for ice cream."

"That's my girl," Patrick said. "I'm going to check on her." He went up the stairs and pushed open Ellery's door. She was snuggled under the covers, sound asleep, with Mr. B next to her. After giving her a kiss, he went across the hall to the master bedroom.

He'd been tempted not to sleep here, since it was still full of Imogen's things. Her perfume, makeup, clothing were all reminders of what he'd lost when she left. He was going to have to come to terms with that. When that would happen, he didn't know. He put his wallet and keys down next to her things and changed into gym shorts and a T-shirt before going downstairs to talk with his brother.

"Beer?" Todd asked when Patrick returned to the living room. Two bottles already sat on the coffee table. Patrick grabbed one and emptied half of it before taking a seat on the couch. "I take it Rachel didn't improve after we talked on the phone?"

"She signed the papers, and that's all that matters." Patrick let himself feel the relief now that he was home. "I don't want to think about her anymore, but I've got a question for you. What'd you mean when you said I take on other people's problems?"

Todd chuckled. "You don't know that's your number one personality trait?"

Coming from anyone else, Todd's response would have pissed Patrick off. "Very funny."

Todd took a drink of beer. "Seriously, you do it all the time. Do you remember when Mom left?"

Like Patrick could forget that day. "Yeah, so?"

"She told you to take care of me, didn't she?"

Patrick shot his brother a look. "How'd you know that?" Their mother had told Patrick that he was a big boy, all of eight years old, and ready to be responsible for his little brother. Her words, the last she'd ever spoken to him, had made an impression. He'd spent the past twenty years trying to live up to them.

"A guess. And you did," Todd said.

"Someone had to." Patrick knew his tone was gruff. "Dad worked all the time and had his own demons."

"True enough," Todd agreed. "But you've never stopped worrying, not even now. I'm an adult with a job and everything."

Patrick shook his head over his brother's job doing community outreach for the local hospital. "I still think you should go have an adventure or two and not settle down here."

"As I've said, I like it here." Todd was unruffled. "You need to accept that and not try to *fix* it."

"I just want you to be happy," Patrick said. That's all he'd ever wanted for his brother. "And if you don't go now—"

"How about you let me worry about that?" Todd said, cutting him off.

Patrick drained his beer as he thought about his brother's words. Taking on people's problems was his personality trait? He'd tried to fix Rachel so many times. He was trying to fix Ellery, but she was a child and that was different. On his SEAL team he had the reputation of efficiently getting to solutions, which he guessed could be considered taking on problems.

Damn. Maybe his kid brother was right.

But Imogen… she didn't seem to fit into his pattern in the same way.

He'd wanted to take on her problems and protect her, but that hadn't been all of it. His feelings for her were more complicated. Or were they really very simple? He wanted to be with her, regardless of anything else.

"What if fixing is the wrong word?" he wondered aloud after several minutes. "What if I want to *share* someone's problems?" He'd always want to fix anything that upset Imogen, since he appeared to be hardwired to do that. But he wanted more from her. He wanted her emotions, her smiles, her body next to his at night, her gentle voice talking to Ellery. He wanted… her everything.

"The person has to be willing to let you share," Todd pointed out as he leaned back in his chair.

Would she be? Patrick glanced up the stairs. He had the perfect excuse to convince Imogen to come home. Her things were up there, and they were still married. She had to return at some point. He'd reach out to her again and invite her to come to the house, and when she did, he'd confess what he was feeling.

It was a scary thought, because she could reject him. There was a chance she would, but he was still going to try. He needed a plan to win her love, a plan he could put in motion soon… because he was done being without her.

22

Imogen read the text from Patrick again. The invitation to collect her things and say goodbye to Ellery arrived two weeks after the trial. She hadn't responded yet. Not because she didn't want to see Ellery or him—not to mention Mr. Bubblesworth—but because the message made it seem that their relationship was over. The official end hopelessly close.

She had to accept that, but since the trial, she'd been trying to reevaluate her life, figure out her new direction. She wanted to be part of Patrick and Ellery's family. And, she had to admit, he'd made an effort to reconnect with her. The messages had come daily. They didn't express his undying love for her, but they showed he cared. Was that enough? If she could be with him, would they have a true marriage?

Or was it all just fiction? She made herself face that likelihood. Without the worry of the trial, she'd had time to think about their relationship. She'd felt blocked out, but maybe he'd just been protecting himself and Ellery from the inevitable separation. She couldn't blame him for that.

His message that day, though, was the push she needed to move on with her life. She still didn't know where she was going, but she couldn't stay in Hartsville. It was too small of a town, and she wouldn't be able to avoid seeing Patrick and Ellery. She needed a fresh start, so she'd load her belongings in her car and go… somewhere. She should be excited about a new future after the past year of fear and stress. At long last she was in control of her life, but it felt meaningless without someone to share it with.

It couldn't be helped. That's what she'd told herself when she consulted a divorce attorney and put the paperwork in motion. Which was another reason for her to see Patrick. She needed his signature to continue the process that would end their marriage. It was time.

She snatched up her phone and sent a text to Patrick. *Would four be a good time to stop by? I promise to be quick.* There. She'd be out of his life by dinnertime.

His response came faster than she imagined possible. *That sounds good.*

At a few minutes before four, she turned onto his road, making her way to the last house. She'd come to love the place in the short time she'd lived there. She pulled into the driveway, promising that wherever she landed in life, she'd buy herself a little house with lace curtains and a front porch. The thought that Patrick and Ellery wouldn't share it with her made her heart sink, but she forced herself to get out of the car. She'd see them, say her goodbyes, and be gone.

Before she reached the porch, the front door opened, and Patrick came out. "Hi, Imogen," he said. He looked good, dark and handsome, but his expression was serious. *He doesn't want me here*, she thought.

"Hello." She climbed the steps to the porch, struggling to keep her composure. "I won't be in your way for long. I do want to see Ellery, though. Is she around?" she asked.

"She's with Todd," he answered, surprising her. "They'll be back in a little while."

"Oh," Imogen said, processing the information. "Well, maybe it's best if she doesn't see me move out."

"She won't want you to go. And neither do I." He took a step closer to her and dropped to one knee.

"What are you..." She couldn't finish her question, since her heart was suddenly full of hope.

He reached for her hands, taking them in his own. "I probably should have let you get all the way in the house, but I can't wait another minute to tell you that I love you."

"You do?" she whispered, hardly able to believe what she was hearing.

He smiled and nodded. "I love you, and I want you to stay with me. I think our marriage can be a real one, and I hope you care enough about me to try."

"I do care about you. I have..." She didn't know where to go with her words next. What he was proposing... wait, he was *proposing*.

"I don't want you to think this is about Ellery," he continued when she fell silent. "Todd said he'd help with her, and we can hire someone, too. This is about the two of us being a couple and sharing all the joys of life."

Happy tears came to her eyes. "I thought you wanted me gone from your life."

"Not at all. Nothing would make me happier than to wake up every morning with you next to me." He released one of her hands and reached in the pocket of his shirt. "I know we're already married, but we didn't do it right the first time."

"We had a lovely wedding," she protested. She cherished her memories of that day.

"But we skipped an important step." He pulled a ring from his pocket and slipped it on her finger with the wedding band. A marquise-cut solitaire diamond sparkled in the light. "I never gave you an engagement ring."

"That's beautiful," she breathed.

"I wish your wedding band were nicer," he said, his fingers touching the gold. "I'll get you a different one. Whatever you like."

"Don't you dare," she said, tugging him to his feet. "I don't want a different ring. I don't want anything but you." She rested her hands on his shoulders, and love that had to be expressed flowed through her. "I love you, Patrick. And I love Ellery. And I love this house. And I would love to be your wife."

"That's a lot of love going around." He lifted one of her hands and kissed her fingers, making her insides melt.

"Think you can handle it?" She put a note of challenge in her voice, but she couldn't keep the smile from her face.

"I'll do my best," he said before lowering his lips to hers.

As he kissed her, she wrapped herself around him, never wanting to let go. This was the life she wanted, her future with him. His hand cradled her head as their bodies pressed together, and she lost herself in the kiss.

"Did she say yes?" Ellery's excited voice came from behind Imogen. Patrick broke the kiss and loosened his hold but didn't let her go.

"I think it was strongly implied," he answered with a glance at Imogen.

"Yes," Imogen said quickly. "I'm officially saying yes."

"Woo-hoo," Ellery yelled and rushed toward them, her arms flung wide. They pulled her into a hug with them.

"Congratulations," Todd said with a grin. Patrick reached to shake his brother's hand and yanked him into the hug as well.

Imogen had been without a family for so long that she felt overwhelmed. She had a man who loved her, a little girl to raise, and even a brother-in-law who was also a friend. The tears flowed down her face.

"Why are you crying?" Patrick asked, looking worried.

"Daddy, she's happy. That's all," Ellery informed him.

"Listen to your daughter," Imogen said, swiping at her cheeks. "She's wise beyond her years."

"We'll have to work on making her your daughter, too," Patrick said.

"Really?" Ellery's heart-shaped face turned from Patrick to Imogen and back. "A mommy who'll never go away?"

"I won't ever leave you," Imogen said, and Ellery started to cry as well.

"We need ice cream, not tears," Todd declared with a laugh. "I'll drive."

EPILOGUE

"Is this good?" Ellery rushed into the master bedroom, swirling around in her floral dress. She did a lovely pirouette and dropped into a curtsy just as her dance teacher had taught her.

"It's perfect. Let me do your hair," Imogen said. Ellery plopped down at the dressing table and fingered Imogen's makeup while Imogen French-braided her hair.

"You've gotten so tall," Imogen commented as she worked. In the past year, Ellery had shot up and become even more of a chatterbox, and the tantrums and anxiety were almost entirely in the past. They'd come a long way in working through her issues, and she was now a happy soon-to-be second grader with a passion for dance class and soccer.

"Can I wear a little blush, since it's a special day?" Ellery had her hand on a makeup brush.

"I guess you could," Imogen said, finishing with her hair and adding a clip with silk rosebuds above Ellery's ear. "Let me see."

Imogen turned Ellery around and evaluated her face. She was a pretty child who would grow up into a beautiful woman in time, not that Imogen was in a rush for that. She picked up a brush and dusted just a smidge of pink blush on the apples of Ellery's cheeks.

"And lipstick?" Ellery asked hopefully.

"Gloss," Imogen said, selecting a rose shade and applying it carefully.

"Eye shadow?" Ellery batted her lashes.

"Do you want to give your daddy a heart attack? You know how he is," Imogen said. Patrick was already worried about his little girl growing up too fast.

"But it's a special day," Ellery said.

"It is that," Imogen agreed. Soon they'd head to the courthouse, where she and Patrick would officially be granted joint custody of Ellery. It would be good to have it recognized legally, but they had become co-parents almost a year ago when she'd accepted his proposal on the front porch of their home.

Since then, Imogen had learned what it was like to be a single parent while worrying about her husband's safety on a mission. Fortunately, he'd only been gone three months, not the six he'd anticipated. The separation was tough, but the homecoming a few months back had been so sweet. Imogen smiled, remembering that night after his arrival. Ellery had worn herself out with excitement and turned in early. Todd had gone home after sharing a celebratory meal with them, saying he didn't want to be a third wheel, and Imogen had gone to work on very little sleep the next day.

And now she had a surprise to share with Patrick, but she'd wait until Ellery was truly theirs to tell him.

"I guess a little," Imogen relented about the eye makeup. "A brush of mascara for today. You can wear more next week for your dance recital."

"Can I really?" Ellery straightened in surprise.

"I think that's the norm. Now, hold still." Imogen brushed the mascara wand lightly over Ellery's ginger eyelashes, darkening them.

"Ladies, are you ready?" Patrick stood in the doorway to the bedroom.

Imogen glanced down at her robe and sent him a pointed look. "Ellery, why don't you wait downstairs with Uncle Todd? We'll be right there."

Ellery scampered off, and a second later they heard her talking to Todd about her dress and makeup.

"Why do I get to stay?" Patrick asked softly but with a knowing grin.

"I'll need help with my zipper, of course." Imogen crossed to the blue sheath dress she'd bought for the occasion. When she undid her robe, his hands were on her immediately, sliding around her waist, and she wondered if he'd notice the subtle changes in her figure she was becoming aware of.

"Is that all?" he asked, dropping a kiss on her shoulder. "I was hoping…"

"Not now," she said and reached for the hanger. "But later…"

"Just what I wanted to hear," he said as she pulled the dress over her head and turned so he could zip her up, his warm fingers trailing along her spine. "I'd like to stay right here with you, but…"

He didn't have to say that he was as excited about the day as she and Ellery were. Imogen knew what it meant to him. Ellery had him wrapped around her little finger, and the two loved each other so much. All signs of their initially rocky relationship were gone.

"I'm ready." Imogen picked up her purse and slipped her feet into a pair of pumps before they went downstairs together.

The four of them headed for the county courthouse to meet with the judge who oversaw family court. The ceremony was simple, taking only minutes, but Ellery, bright-eyed, clung to Imogen's and Patrick's hands like they were lifelines as the judge declared that they had joint custody of her.

"We're a family," Ellery said, dancing around them.

Imogen wanted to say that they always had been, but she understood how important those words were for Ellery, a once-abandoned child who now had two parents who loved her.

"Congratulations," Anita from Child Protective Services said. She and a few others had attended the ceremony. "It makes us so happy at CPS when families are made whole. The best of luck to you."

Imogen and Patrick accepted the well-wishes of others as they made their way out of the courtroom with Ellery between them.

"What next, honey?" Patrick looked down at his daughter. "I know you have a plan."

"Could we have lunch at the Hartsville Café to celebrate?" she asked, giving her father her sweetest smile, one he couldn't resist. Not that he would, because this was a day to rejoice.

"I think we can do that." Patrick turned to his brother. "Can you join us?"

"I took the whole day off work," he said. "I'd love to. Come on, Ellery." He took his niece's hand and moved ahead of Patrick and Imogen. "I want to be seen walking down the street with the prettiest girl in Hartsville."

Imogen looped her arm through Patrick's when they reached the street and turned toward the same little restaurant where they'd eaten after their wedding.

"Seems appropriate to go there," he said. "It must be our happy place."

"Yes. And… we have one more thing to celebrate." Imogen sent him a sidelong look. This was the right moment to tell him her secret. She was glad she'd waited until now.

"We do?" he asked, looking perplexed. "I'm married to a beautiful woman I love so much, and together we have a very happy daughter." He nodded to where Ellery was skipping along ahead of them with Todd. "What else could there be?"

"Do you have enough love to share with another child?" She couldn't keep the smile away any longer.

"Do I…" He stopped, turning her to face him. "Are you pregnant, sweetheart?"

"I am… we are," she said, feeling a blush come to her cheeks. "I think the baby was conceived the night you returned from your mission." She was pretty sure of that after consulting a calendar online, and somehow it made the baby growing in her womb even more special.

"I knew that was a very good day," he murmured as he pulled her closer to him. "And don't worry. I've got plenty of love for everyone."

He kissed her then, and she had no reason to worry about anything at all.

END OF THE SEAL'S CONVENIENT WIFE

HARTSVILLE'S SEAL HEROES BOOK ONE

PS: Do you love hot blooded SEALS? Turn the page for an exclusive free book offer and exclusive extracts from *The SEAL's Surprise Baby* and *Protecting His Pregnant Lover*.

FREE BOOK OFFER

Read FIVE full-length romances by USA Today best-selling author Leslie North for FREE! Over 600+ pages of best-selling romance with hundreds of FIVE STAR REVIEWS!

<u>Sign-up to her mailing list and get your FREE books</u>

THANK YOU!

Thank you so much for purchasing my book. It's hard for me to put into words how much I appreciate my readers. If you enjoyed this book, please remember to leave a review. Reviews are crucial for an author's success and I would greatly appreciate it if you took the time to review the book. I love hearing from you!

You can connect with me on:

MAKE AN AUTHOR'S DAY

There's nothing better than reading great reviews from readers like yourself, but there's more to it than simply putting a smile on my face. As an independent author, I don't have the financial might of a big NYC publishing house or the clout to get in Oprah's book club. What I do have, as my not-so-secret weapon is you, my awesome readers!

If you enjoyed this book, I'd be incredibly grateful if you could leave a quick review. No matter the length (short is fine!), your review will help this series get the exposure it needs to grow and make it into the hands of other awesome readers. Plus, reading your kind reviews is often the highlight of my day, so please be sure to let me know what you loved most about this book.

ABOUT LESLIE

Leslie North is the USA Today Bestselling pen name for a critically-acclaimed author of women's contemporary romance and fiction. The anonymity gives her the perfect opportunity to paint with her full artistic palette, especially in the romance and erotic fantasy genres.

Find your next Leslie North book visit LeslieNorthBooks.com or choose:

PS: Want sneak peeks, giveaways, ARC offers, fun extras and plenty of pictures of bad boys? Join my Facebook group, Leslie's Lovelies!

BLURB

Navy SEAL Anderson Park and agency operative Violet DiPaula didn't like each other, but that didn't diminish the spark between them. On a mission together in Russia, they gave in to the red-hot chemistry between them. Anderson is always prepared, but nothing could have prepared him for returning from a mission more than a year later and learning that their one night of passion left Violet pregnant. Anderson's good at most things, but he knows he'll be a lousy father. Now Violet and his five-month-old son are in danger, and he can't abandon them. As much as Anderson knows he's not cut out for family life, he can't avoid his protective instincts toward Violet and Nate. Before he knows it, he also can't keep his heart from feeling things he's never felt before…

If it were just Violet on the run, she'd be fine. But she has Nate, and that changes everything. Violet has always taken care of herself, and it's no easy task allowing Anderson to help her and their son. She doesn't *need* a man, but the safe house is her undoing. It just all seems so cozy, and having a sexy SEAL around morning, noon, and night isn't the worst thing that's ever happened. No matter how many times Violet reminds herself she doesn't need a thing from Anderson, as the danger increases and they must rely on each other more and more, she finds herself falling hard. If they survive the Russian mob, can their love survive as well?

Grab your copy of *The SEAL's Surprise Baby*
<u>www.LeslieNorthBooks.com</u>

EXCERPT

Chapter One

"What?" Anderson said, trying to keep his mouth from hanging open. He couldn't have heard her correctly. Maybe the sound of the breeze moving through leaves was messing with his hearing. Had she just declared that the baby in her arms was his?

"You have a son," Violet repeated, smoothing a hand over the boy's hair. "His name is Nate."

"Nate." Anderson spoke the word slowly, waiting for his brain to catch up with Violet's announcement.

"Nathan Anderson DiPaula," she said. That was her last name. Instinct made him want to argue the point. If the kid was his, the boy's name should be Nathan Park.

No. Wait a minute.

"He can't be mine. I never…" Never what? Never let my swimmers out without a safety net? No SEAL worth his salt did, in Anderson's opinion. He didn't have unprotected sex—ever. But he looked at the boy with his dark hair and eyes and wondered. Was it possible?

"Do you mind if we come in?" Violet asked, glancing behind her. "I don't want to talk about… certain things standing on your porch."

"Yeah… sure," Anderson muttered and stood aside to let her—and the baby—by. He'd been enjoying some time alone, recovering from his last mission, when Violet had unexpectedly knocked on his door. He walked ahead of her into the living room, gesturing to the couch he'd been napping on. Any sense of peace or relaxation he'd found had vanished the instant he saw her.

They'd parted fourteen months ago at Ramstein Air Base in Germany after an emergency extraction from the assignment they'd been on together in Moscow. When he'd thought of her since, it had been with a sense of irritation. Everything about her got under his skin. Her fearless attitude, her cool intelligence, her sexy body.

Having a baby hadn't changed that much. Her slim-fitting jeans and pink tank top revealed the curves he'd been unable to resist that last night in Russia. A fateful night, if what she said was true and the kid was his. He focused on the boy. He had fine dark hair that fell over a high forehead and eyes darker than his mother's. Hers always seemed to glow with a sort of inner light.

The baby's chubby hands reached out and yanked on Violet's chestnut hair.

"We talked about this, little man. No pulling Mama's hair," she said as she smiled at Nate and gently removed the locks from his fist. "Let me find you a toy." With one hand, she dug in the bag she'd dropped at her feet. "How about this?" She offered the boy a book made from fabric.

"Does he like that?" Anderson asked, finding his voice.

"It's a favorite. I think he'll be a scholar."

"Like his mother," he said. She was one of the smartest people he knew. He hadn't always liked her, but he'd respected her ability to analyze data and make projections. He was good at that, too, but her skill far surpassed his.

"And Daddy," she added, shooting him a look.

Anderson's scholarship was hard won, since he'd come from damn close to nothing. He'd risen above his beginnings, doing more than anyone expected from him, but shit, had he ended up just like his parents with an unplanned kid? He had to get his head around the idea of having a baby.

"How'd this happen?" he blurted out.

"The usual way, Anderson. We had sex." She gave him a look that said, *Try to deny it*. "Do I have to explain the biology?"

"I get that part, but I also know there was a condom involved." He wasn't the type to take risks, ever. Not even back when he'd been a randy sixteen-year-old—and certainly not a year and change ago.

She lifted her shoulders an inch. "Ninety-eight percent effective when used correctly, according to the sources I checked. That leaves a two in one hundred chance."

"Thanks, I can do the math," Anderson said, working to keep the sharpness from his voice. "How old is he?"

"Five months. I just got confirmation a few days ago that you were back in the States," she added, as if anticipating his next question.

"Right." Anderson couldn't stop studying the child, looking for signs of himself in the set of his mouth and his laugh as the baby turned the pages in the book.

"You were gone on a long deployment, from what I could find out," she continued.

"You checked?" With her security clearance and connections in the intelligence world, she would have been able to find out that he was deployed. She might even have uncovered where he'd been, but she'd made no move to contact him. At least, not that he knew of.

"I did," she admitted as she lowered the boy to the floor so that he sat supported against her legs. He seemed able to sit up pretty well on his own. Maybe he was an advanced little guy, Anderson thought, and then the kid stuck half the cloth book in his mouth. Guess not.

"So you waited for me to be on leave to drop this bomb," he said, watching as she offered the baby a set of plastic keys in exchange for the now-wet book. She tilted her face toward Anderson before speaking.

"I waited because I wasn't sure I'd tell you at all." Those eyes that seemed to have their own light stared into his. "I don't need you. I can raise him on my own and give him everything a child needs."

"Except a father," he pointed out, fully aware of the irony of his words. His father had been a crook and a wannabe con artist. Not exactly daddy-of-the-year material. Anderson's grandfather hadn't been any better. Fatherhood wasn't in his genes.

"I grew up without one," Violet retorted. "It's never held me back."

That much was true. She'd never been daunted by anything. Not that he'd seen. But raising a kid on her own had to be tough.

Did that mean he wanted to be involved? Hell, he didn't know the answer to that.

"So why'd you show up at my door?" he asked, trying to understand her motive.

"I decided you had a right to know," she said, touching the boy's head. "And he's so sweet. I couldn't live with myself if you didn't have the opportunity to experience that." She cleared her throat, and he felt there was something she wasn't saying. "So that's why I'm here."

He believed her, but something didn't add up in his head. He let a minute pass in silence while he analyzed her words. Then he said, "You would have known you were pregnant before I was deployed on my last mission."

"That's true. I suppose I should explain a little more about that," she said. "I've never been regular, you know what I mean?" He nodded, not wanting to get into a discussion of female issues. "So I was almost five months pregnant before I let myself believe it. When my clothes stopped fitting, I could no longer deny the reality, so I took a test and saw the doctor."

"You weren't sick?" Didn't women know these things? There were signs, or so he'd always heard.

"Not a day. And I wasn't tired either, like so many women say they are. It was an easy pregnancy." She lifted the baby back onto her lap. "Anyway, by the time I came to terms with it, you'd shipped out— and I'd thought that was just as well, since we don't..." Her mouth closed into a firm line.

"Get along," he supplied. Both their working and personal relationships had been infused with tension, some of it sexual, but much of it a battle of wills.

"Right." She swallowed, a surprising show of nerves on her part. "But I'm here now to give you a choice. Your son can be part of your life or not. If you decide you want nothing to do with him, I'll never bother you again."

Anderson started to say *If he's mine*, and stopped himself. He had no reason to doubt her assertion, and the time frame worked. The kid… Nate… was his. Did Anderson want to be a father? He had never planned on it. But he also didn't shirk his responsibilities. But, Jesus, it was a hell of a decision to be asked to make out of the blue.

He'd seen enough careless and irresponsible behavior from his own parents to know he didn't want to emulate that. But could he do this? Could he be a dad? And what would that mean for him and Violet? He saw a future fraught with battles, which was not how he wanted to live.

But he'd fathered a kid, and that meant something. He'd pay child support. The Navy would help him set that up. Beyond the monetary, though… he didn't know. His mind swirled, refusing to go in any coherent direction.

"Got it. Message received," Violet said and got to her feet, interpreting his silence as refusal. She slung her bag over her shoulder and cuddled Nate close to her body.

Anderson had seen her in slinky dresses meant for nightclubs and in business suits, but she'd never looked more beautiful than she did then. Her clothes were casual, her hair mussed, but her face, body, and attitude got to him just as much as they always had.

And he knew that he didn't want her or his son to walk out his door. Not until he'd had a chance to think this through.

"Wait," he said, jumping up and moving to be in front of her. "You've got to give me a little—"

The sound of bullets from an automatic weapon suddenly filled the air. Instinct made Anderson wrap his arms around Violet and Nate and take them to the floor with him. Everything in him said to protect them above all else. He landed on his back, taking the brunt of the impact, and then rolled with them to use his body as a shield.

The hail of bullets ended, leaving a car alarm blaring in the street. He eased up, checking his surroundings.

"Is he…?" For the first time, Anderson touched his son. It was inadvertent, a simple hand to the boy's cheek, but it was soft, warm, and captivating.

"He's fine," Violet said, her voice shaky. "What happened?"

"Not sure. Stay down," he said as he rose into a crouch and made his way to the window. He looked through the glass pane and saw the sedan Violet must have arrived in riddled with bullet holes. A rock hurtled toward the house as a black SUV peeled out and careened down the road, almost hitting Anderson's mailbox. He took another minute to scan the area before standing. When he did, he bumped into Violet. Why had she joined him at the window? He should have known she wouldn't stay still—but the kid.

Anderson turned. Nate lay on his back on the carpet, moving his limbs and babbling to himself, undisturbed by anything that was happening.

"There's a note," Violet said, pointing through the window to where the rock had landed on his porch.

"I'll get it." He didn't bother to tell her to stay in the house. It was a waste of breath.

Anderson stepped onto the porch to retrieve the note. Once he was back inside, he unfolded it and scanned the words. Violet leaned in to see it, her hair brushing against his arm.

"My God," she muttered in Russian, speaking in the language of the note.

His language skills were on par with hers, and he had no trouble understanding the threat.

Next time, you'll be in the car.

"I didn't think…" She made her way back to the couch, scooped up Nate, and sat down heavily.

Didn't think what? Violet was shaken… but not surprised. What was going on? He studied her. Her head was bent over the baby's, and her body seemed to be folded inward. He needed to break through the walls she was constructing and get her to talk.

"Let me take him," Anderson said, walking toward her and reaching for his son. His request jolted her.

Violet glanced up, her eyes unfocused for a second, before handing Nate over. Anderson felt awkward for a minute as he tried to mimic how she'd carried the baby, but he soon figured out to rest Nate against his chest. He paced the room, keeping an eye on the street out front, but he didn't expect them to return so soon since they'd delivered their message. "Explain what you know," he said. "Don't leave anything out."

"There was a data breach two months ago," she began after the tiniest hesitation, "not long after I went back to work following my maternity leave." Her job for a government agency wasn't the kind she could discuss with most people, but he already knew about it. He'd been her protector, a glorified babysitter, really, while she'd been on assignment in Moscow.

"The leak had to do with information you collected in Russia," he guessed.

She nodded. "It revealed some of the surveillance and analysis and who conducted it."

"And your bosses didn't react." That surprised him. They were usually protective of their assets, and that's how they would view Violet.

"It was deemed minor with minimal exposure, but…"

"But what?" he demanded, keeping his voice level. Nate seemed to be dozing, cuddled into him, and he didn't want to spook the boy.

"I've had a few strange incidents since," she said, her fingers twisting the edge of her shirt. "Little things. Someone following too close behind my car. An unexpected package on my doorstep."

"What was in it?" Anderson paused in his pacing.

"Russian nesting dolls." She gave him a wry smile. "A warning, no doubt. I think someone's toying with me, but I don't know why."

The bullet-filled hunk of metal on the street was way past a warning. Fortunately, he lived on a country lane outside town and had no immediate neighbors. No one would be freaking out and calling the police. At least not yet. He had a little time for his mind to tick over what he knew. He didn't like any of it.

"We need to get out of here," he said after a minute spent analyzing their best course of action.

"What? Now?" She stood, her body reacting to his suggestion.

"Yeah," he said, "unless you want to wait around for them to come back." She was too smart for that not to be obvious to her.

She glanced out the window. "I should report this to my supervisor."

"Did you report the other things?" he demanded.

"Of course." She reached into her bag and pulled out her phone.

"And what did they do?" he asked before she could dial.

"Nothing, which didn't really surprise me—who knows; they might have more information than I do." Her fingers stilled over the buttons. Since her area of expertise was risk analysis, he found it odd that anyone had doubted her assessment. "The threat seemed as though it originated from a minor source with minimal exposure, same as the original data breach. I've followed the usual protocols for enhanced threat, though."

How much more complicated was that with a child to care for? Anderson didn't want to think about it. He would later, after they were in a safe location.

"My car's in the garage," he said, ready to take action. "Let's roll."

"Wait. I can't go on the run with a baby. All I have for him is what's in this bag. Let me go home and—"

He cut her off. "No. Your place isn't going to be safe." He knew he was right about that, but fleeing a threat with a baby—with his son—wasn't the way he wanted to spend his first day as a dad.

"I…" She only hesitated a couple of seconds; he could see her evaluating the situation in her head, assessing risks and options. "Okay. You're right." She grabbed the bag and took Nate from Anderson. "Car seat?"

"What?" It was his turn to be surprised.

"Kids have to ride in a car seat for safety," she explained. "We'll need to get it from my car if it's not damaged."

He wanted to argue that their situation was inherently unsafe, but her jaw had a stubborn set he remembered well. "I'll get it. You can reach the garage by going through the kitchen."

He pointed the way before pulling jackets from his hall closet and stuffing them into a tactical bag he always kept packed. A minute later he yanked the door of the bullet-riddled car open to retrieve the car seat. He had no idea how to manage the thing, but he managed to detach it and hauled it to the garage.

"Let me," she said, taking it and quickly strapping it down while he held Nate. He watched her run her finger over a notch in the plastic where a bullet had sliced through. "Good thing he wasn't..." She didn't need to finish the sentence.

"We need to move," Anderson said to hurry her along. Thirty seconds later, he backed out of his garage and headed in the opposite direction from where the black SUV had gone. He didn't want to run into whoever had been at the wheel with Violet and Nate in the car.

The problem was he had no idea where the hell they were going.

Grab your copy of *The SEAL's Surprise Baby*
www.LeslieNorthBooks.com

BLURB

Self-proclaimed nerd Olive Owen can't believe it when Levon Asher, sexy, nothing-but-muscle Navy SEAL admits to having had a crush on her in high school. She hasn't seen him in ten years, and reconnecting with him at their high school reunion is a bit of a surprise. A bigger surprise is that after one night of passionate love-making, Olive is pregnant, and Levon has long since left town on a final SEAL mission. When he returns seven months later, he's a member of the private security group Southern Soldiers of Fortune, who are in town for a joint operation with the local police to stop a gang from infiltrating the school where Olive works. When Olive accidentally stumbles onto a gang meeting, the threats on her doorstep leave no doubt —she's being targeted. And when she agrees to move in with Levon for her own safety, it soon becomes clear her heart is in danger too.

Knowing Olive's at risk is driving Levon crazy. He realizes he's being overbearing, but he just can't stop himself. The thought of anything happening to her or his unborn child is enough to make him more than a little controlling. But what's safer—keeping her close, where he can protect her, or pushing her back, out of harm's way? He needs Olive to be okay, but his impulses are giving him mixed signals even as the clock starts counting down to a confrontation with the gang. A shocking reveal of a gang member's identity could drive Olive away from Levon for good, leaving him wondering if solving the crime will come too late to resolve the mystery that matters most to him—how to hold on to Olive's heart.

Grab your copy of *Protecting His Pregnant Lover* (Southern Soldiers of Fortune Book One) from www.LeslieNorthBooks.com

EXCERPT

Chapter One

Levon Asher melted back against the wall inside the gym at Harper's Forge High, breathing in the familiar dust and lingering scent of sweaty socks. He scouted out the room, taking in the faces of strangers who were once his friends. He took a sip of spiked punch, and grimaced. Every muscle in his mouth came together in a pucker that would have spat the concoction back out if his manners didn't dictate otherwise. He didn't remember the rum-punch combo tasting this bad when he was in high school; granted, he tended to stick to beer.

Why was he here again?

Loud voices off to the side caught his attention and he turned to see a group of grown men standing on the bleachers and jostling each other as they handed out cans of beer; each voice getting louder.

That would be his former football team minus Levon, of course, because he was currently buried up against the wall. "This isn't a special-ops mission, it's my high school reunion," he reminded himself as he stepped away from the wall. Or maybe he could simply call this mission a fail and get out before anyone noticed him.

"Asher! Get your ass over here and drink with *us!*" one of his old teammates hollered across the other conversations in the room. Levon froze, lifted his Solo cup in acknowledgement, then set it aside and moved through the crowd toward them hoping they'd offer him a beer.

When he joined them, he gratefully took a beer hiding his frown when he realized it was warm. Popping the tab, he took a sip appreciating that it wasn't the punch but wishing it was many degrees cooler. Much like outside.

Ordinarily, their high school reunion would have been held in June but this was the school's diamond jubilee and the school board had decided to combine the two events—probably to save money—so here he was in his high school gym at the end of February with decorations that looked like leftovers from the school's Valentine's Day dance.

An elbow to his side caught his attention and he tried to concentrate on what his former teammates were talking about and instantly regretted it.

"How can it be that every single cheerleader let herself go?" one of the ex-jocks chimed in, elbowing Levon again, and compelling him to look around the room. He couldn't understand what they were complaining about. They were all a little older, but as far as he could tell, no one had seemed to have let themselves go.

He looked around at the other players trying to put names to faces but failing more than succeeding. Finally, he gave up and let his gaze fall to the stick-on name tags trying to match the names to the faces of his former teammates. Okay, clearly some of us had changed and not for the better, he thought to himself. The banter continued and what may have been harmless locker room talk when they were in high school was bordering on the offensive now.

Levon sipped his beer, counting the seconds until he could make his excuses to get away. He was back in town for a job interview, and when he'd realized the timing of his ten-year reunion, he'd felt nostalgic enough to give it a try. That had been a big mistake. He had nothing in common with these guys anymore.

"Hey, check it out." One of the guys nudged him, Randy according to his name tag, and the others quieted. "Why don't we all make a bet on which of the nerdy chicks turned out hot? There's always gotta be one, right?"

"What about that little mousy chick you had for your lab partner, Asher? She skipped a grade or two, but she still graduated with us, didn't she?" chimed in Chad, who had been their Center.

Levon didn't reply. In truth, his thoughts had strayed to Olive Owen more than once tonight... and all the nights leading up to the reunion... but he hadn't seen her yet. He doubted if she'd come. Olive had always been the smartest person he knew; definitely too smart to get caught up in—

One of the jocks wolf-whistled, and the others craned to look. If this was the direction the evening was going it, Levon was out. His eyes sought out the nearest exit—or at least, tried to.

Standing in the middle of the crowded gym was one of the most gorgeous women he had ever seen. Her head was turned slightly, but he saw enough of her to mark her big eyes, her full lips, her neat little nose. Chocolate brown curls cascaded down the pale length of her swan-like neck and tumbled across bare shoulders. Her dress was a dark, muted shade of wine red; it looked simple and inexpensive, but then, a beauty with those long, alabaster legs, those calves, those curves in all the right places, could make even a garbage bag look like the height of elegance.

For the first time that evening, Levon took real interest in his surroundings. Something stirred to life in him as he assessed this woman from afar. God, he had always loved a girl with curly hair, ever since unassuming Olive tripped into the seat beside his own in sophomore year—

The woman turned, her gaze flickering over the group of men hunched like vultures above the rest of them. Levon was glad for his military posture in that moment, when he noticed the way her look of passing curiosity immediately cooled upon realizing who made up the ranks on the bleachers. She fished in her purse for something and withdrew a black, spindly pair of glasses, which she pushed home along the bridge of her nose. She didn't bother looking in their direction again.

His teammates realized her identity the same instant he did. Levon hated the fact that he hadn't realized it sooner.

"I knew it! It's her!" Randy crowed. "What's-her-name."

"Olive." Her name was a welcome surprise on Levon's tongue. *Olive.* He had only ever said it out loud as a boy; now, hearing his gruff acknowledgement of her sent a thrill through him, making her all the more a woman now that he was a man.

"Olive!" Randy slapped him on the back. "Yo! What did I tell you? That girl is *banging.* I knew she'd get hot eventually!"

"Olive has always been hot." Levon downed the rest of his beer, crumpled the can like it was tinfoil, and resisted the urge to contour it to Randy's face. "Wish I could say it was nice catching up. Later." He made sure his *later* took on the tone of *never.*

"What the hell? Asher!" Chad called after him as Levon exited the bleachers.

"You just gonna drink our beer and take off?" Randy demanded. "Big, tough SEAL!"

Levon threw a look over his shoulder and the group visibly shrank under his gaze. He continued down the bleachers. He was far more interested in the woman who had managed to vanish from sight in the moments he'd been distracted. Levon cursed under his breath. He deposited his empty dutifully in the recycling bin, grabbed his coat, and then ran a hand through his hair. It was still short by civilian standards, but it had grown out since he'd been on leave and made him uncomfortable. He was so used to regulations that it seemed a betrayal to let anything about his appearance slip below standards. Maybe he'd go back to his hotel room tonight, enjoy one more solitary beer, and buzz it himself.

Seemed as good an excuse as any to get the hell out of here.

Levon pocketed his big hands and wandered the darkened hallways of the old high school on his way out... or at least, what he *thought* was his way out. Evidently the school had scrounged up some funds to renovate, because the more he wandered, the more he realized he had no idea where he was. A few more turns spat him out in an older section that he immediately recognized as the science wing.

Levon wasted no time making for the first lighted door; he had wasted enough time trying to escape these funhouse halls already. The new renovations were really starting to mess with his nostalgia. Thankfully, one of the science teachers appeared to be putting in some after-hours. He rapped on the door with his knuckles, then let himself in without awaiting a response. "Hi. Sorry. I'm here for the reunion, I just got turned around with all the—"

What was turning out to be a pretty lame explanation died mid-delivery in his throat when, at the lab table closest to him, a styled head of curly hair lifted, and a pair of startled eyes blinked in shock. The makeup bag the woman had been fishing for in her purse flew out of her hand and spilled its contents on the floor between them.

"Ah, crap, I'm sorry." Levon knelt to recover the woman's effects, and was surprised when his questing fingers brushed a smaller pair that joined him. "I shouldn't have just busted in like that."

"It's all right… really, I… *ow!*" The woman's head knocked against his as they leaned forward to stand in the same moment. Levon caught hold of her before she could fall back to the ground; he knew he had a thick skull, and wasn't exactly sure how hard they had collided. It was just his luck to head-butt Olive Owen, but he could only hope she wasn't seriously hurt.

Olive Owen. The beauty in his arms gazed up at him; then, to his surprise and great relief, she laughed. Hopefully that wasn't a symptom of a concussion. "Levon Asher? Wow, uh, I thought that might've been you I saw earlier on the bleachers in the gym, but wasn't sure. Didn't expect to see you here. You didn't come to the five-year reunion."

"No," he said, fumbling for words, distracted by how good she felt in his arms. Or maybe that awful rum punch he'd had before was more potent than he'd thought. Whatever the reason, he was currently making an ass out of himself. He let her go and stepped back, watching her from under his lashes. Man, up close, she looked even better than before, those perfect cheekbones of hers all glowing and rosy. He wondered if maybe Olive had enjoyed a bit too much punch herself.

"It's good to see you," he said, for lack of anything better. "You look great. If science class had been at all like this, I wouldn't have skipped so often." His throat constricted with embarrassment. Damn. *Way to be not smooth, dude.* Heat blasted up his face. "I mean, not that you didn't look great back then. I mean…"

She snorted and pushed those glasses higher up her nose again. For some reason, it made her look even hotter. Kind of a sexy librarian vibe going on. Or maybe that was Levon's overtaxed mind. Exactly how many drinks had he had again? "I know what you mean," Olive said at last, letting him off the hook, though the air between them still seemed to sizzle. "Anyway, you didn't skip *that* often."

She crossed her arms over her chest, thrusting those perky boobs of hers higher and crap. Now all Levon seemed to be able to see was that. Those. Them. His night was suddenly going from bad to worse. Or better to best, depending on how you looked at it. If Olive noticed his pointed perusal at least she didn't mention it.

"I tried not to," he said, his deep voice even gruffer than usual as he tried to force his attention away from her body and back to her eyes. It wasn't usually this much of a strain to hold himself together and avoid tripping over his tongue. He needed to get laid. That was it. He'd been too long without a woman. That had to explain his crazy urge to pull his old lab partner Olive into his arms and take her right there on the science room floor, right? Or, given the way his libido seemed to have taken over his verbal responses, maybe not. Before he could stop himself, he said, "Not when my lab partner was so—"

"Helpful? When it came to studying for the quizzes?" she suggested, raising a dark brow at him. "I remember spending many nights doing that together. Afternoons and mornings too. In fact, we seemed to do nothing but study back then."

Levon could think of lots of activities he'd like to do with Olive Owen now that didn't involve any kind of textbooks or papers. He tried to hide the desire pulsing through his bloodstream—and failed miserably, if the flat look she gave him was any indication. "Uh, yeah," he managed to say at last. God, he needed to contain his crazy reactions to her before he messed this up even more. He'd spent years fantasizing about meeting her again and now that he finally had his chance, he was screwing it up. *Get your shit together, dude.* Levon scowled down at the floor and concentrated on ship schematics and battlefield diagrams, anything to cool the ardor boiling within him. "I was thinking of a different word."

"Really?" Olive tapped the toe of her pump on the floor, clearly having had enough of his crap. He remembered her doing that back when they were in school too. She'd never put up with his excuses back then either. Always pushing him to do his best, always believing he could do better, be better. Honestly, she'd been one of the few people who didn't let him skate by because of his looks and his charm. Levon wasn't sure he'd be where he was without Olive's help. A new emotion, gratitude, joined the vibrant attraction humming through him like an electric charge. Her snarky response only increased his interest. Her dark eyes were twinkling and the pink in her cheeks had darkened. If Levon didn't know better, he'd think she was flirting with him—that she was just as turned on by this volatile chemistry between them as he was. But that couldn't be right, could it? Olive back in high school had been all work and no play. Looking at her now though, all sexy and sophisticated, maybe more than her appearance had changed. She gave him a tiny half-smile full of smolder and said, "What word is that?"

He tried to come up with an equally provocative response, but his mind was too preoccupied with how she looked, how she smelled, how she might taste if he kissed her. Levon played it off with a shrug, blaming his dyslexia again because it was as good an excuse as any. "You know me. Takes me a while to think of what to say." *Especially with you so close.*

"I'll wait." She tilted her head, exposing that delectable throat of hers and, now all he could think about was nuzzling that spot right beneath her ear. Damn, he had it bad for Olive Owen and that wasn't good. "I'm good at waiting."

"I remember," he said quietly, memories of their long study sessions back in high school replaying in his head. "Uh, how about we get out of here and you let me buy you a drink and we can talk about the old days?"

"The old days?" Olive narrowed her gaze on him a moment as if considering his request, her red lips compressed. For a long moment he thought she might turn him down, and Levon was surprised by how disappointed that prospect made him. Then she smiled and nodded. "Sure. I guess I've been waiting long enough to see how you turned out. Tonight, I get my answer. Where should we go?"

"Is the Rusty Spike still open?" he asked, waiting while she locked up her classroom, then following her to the exit. "It's been a while since I've been in town."

"Yeah, it's still there," Olive said, pushing out into the cool night. The parking lot and his waiting truck were not far away. "Still a total dive too."

"If there's somewhere else you want to go…"

"No. The Rusty Spike is fine. Not much else to choose from around here," she said, walking beside him down the sidewalk, the yellowish glow from the streetlights catching fire in the highlights running through her chocolate-colored curls. Levon felt an insane urge to run his fingers through them to see if they felt as soft as they looked, but he didn't think Olive would appreciate him messing up her fancy new do.

"Which car is yours?" she asked, jarring him out of his inappropriate thoughts.

"Oh, that one," he said, pointing to the shiny black extended cab Ford. It was a nice ride, with plenty of leg room for him and all the bells and whistles inside. If he'd been in the market for a vehicle of his own, this would be the one he'd get. As it was, he wouldn't be in town long enough to do much driving. He'd be off on his last SEAL mission soon enough. "It's a rental."

"Nice."

He clicked the button on the key fob and the lights flickered as the doors clicked open. Olive opened the passenger side door before Levon could get there to do it for her and climbed into her seat, buckling her seatbelt while he walked around the front of the truck and slid in behind the wheel. Soon he'd cranked the engine and pulled out of the lot, heading for the only bar in town. While he drove, awkward silence descended between them again, until Olive started chatting about the people at the reunion. He only half-listened, not particularly interested in any of the attendees. Other than her.

They slowed for a red light and she giggled. An honest to God giggle, and the husky sound went straight to Levon's groin. So much for playing it cool. He shifted in his seat, glad his longer shirt covered any embarrassing situations down below. Olive ran a hand through her hair, then looked over at him. "Sorry. I think I might've had too much punch back at the gym."

Me too. Levon bit back the words and frowned, punching the accelerator harder than necessary once the light turned green. Moments later, they arrived at the bar and he pulled into an open spot near the end of the row in the gravel lot. This time he got out and went around to help Olive out of the truck. The height meant her skirt rode up a bit as she stepped down, giving him a glimpse of slim thighs and shapely calves and damn if he couldn't stop thinking about those legs wrapped around his waist as he drove into her warm wetness over and over again.

Shit.

"Thanks," Olive said, her hand still in his as she stood before him, their eyes locked and their breath hitching. *Oh boy.* Then she stepped back and smoothed her hand down her dress. "We should, um, get inside and get a table. The place fills up quick."

Right. They were here to have a drink and get reacquainted, not screw in the parking lot. The sooner Levon remembered that, the better. Still, as he followed her into the dark, noisy bar, he couldn't help noticing the sway of her hips as she walked. Olive Owen had definitely grown up.

Luckily, there were two seats still open at the end of the bar by the pool tables and they took a seat, Levon ordering a dark lager and Olive sticking with sparkling water this time.

"So," he said after taking a long swig from his bottle to quench his parched throat. "What have you been up to since high school?"

"Well, college, of course. Then coming back here and getting a job teaching science."

"Really?" At her grin, he connected the dots. "Wait, are you saying you teach at Harper's Forge High now?"

"Yep. In fact, that classroom you barged into earlier is mine."

"Wow." Levon chuckled, some of the tension knotting between his shoulder blades easing. "Imagine that. Olive Owen taking over our old classroom."

"It's Miss Owen now." She winked at him and the room seemed to get a little hotter. Levon resisted the urge to run his finger beneath the collar of his shirt. "And yes. The sophomores are mine."

Amidst the clack of pool balls from the tables nearby and the drone of conversation around them, he and Olive spent the next hour or so catching up. He told her as much as he could about his time in the Navy and his training for the SEALs, and she talked about her life in their small hometown. Eventually, the alcohol in his system and the lack of food in his stomach created a nice buzz that chased away any remaining inhibitions he might have had. Then again, the three ales he'd downed, on top of what he'd had before in the gym, didn't hurt either.

The sound of Olive's voice was nice, soothing, sexy. He was happy just to listen to her talk. Besides he didn't really have more to say.

Or maybe he did.

The simmering want in his blood rolled into a full boil and he found himself reaching over to take her hand. It probably wasn't the wisest move ever, but hell if he could make himself care anymore. Time reduced to only the now, only this woman, this night, this moment.

He leaned closer to Olive, and whispered near her ear to be heard over the din in the room, "What do you say we continue this somewhere more private?"

Levon didn't imagine the slight shiver that ran through her body, or the heat in her gaze as her eyes met his. Yep. She wanted him too. No doubt about it. It might have been a while since he'd been with a woman, but a man never forgot a look like that.

Olive licked her lips and he tracked the tiny movement, thinking about all the places he'd love to have her use that cute pink tongue on him.

"Let's go," she said, and that was all he needed to hear.

After slapping a fifty down on the bar top for what was probably twenty dollars' worth of drinks, they grabbed their coats and Levon took Olive's hand and all but ran out of the bar with her, not caring that people might talk behind their backs. It was a small town after all. And sure as hell not caring if he seemed way too eager to be with her. Right now, his entire universe consisted of Olive Owen and he didn't care who knew it.

Between kisses and caresses, they somehow made it to his truck. In a tangle of limbs and lust, they climbed inside. The cab of the truck was bigger than most, but still not ideal for making love. Still, they made it work. He quickly turned the ignition to "on" and the cab soon filled with heat even though he was fairly sure they wouldn't need it. Levon tore off his tie and button-down shirt, popping a few buttons along the way, while Olive tugged her burgundy sheath dress off over her head, leaving her in nothing but a lacy black bra and matching panties. She straddled him in the seat, the warmth between her legs brushing over his khaki-covered hard cock, and Levon was lost.

He couldn't get enough of her. Forget the punch or the beer or anything else.

Olive was by far the most intoxicating thing tonight.

Soon her bra was gone and he had those fabulous breasts of hers in his palms, their soft weight filling his hands perfectly as he teased her taut nipples with his fingers and thumbs before taking each one into his mouth in turn, making her moan and writhe against him again.

Next he slid her panties down and off her legs, while she fiddled with his belt and unzipped his pants to take him firmly in hand. It took all his hard-won willpower not to come instantly at the contact of her warm skin against him, but somehow he managed. Man, he wanted her like he hadn't wanted anyone in a long time, maybe ever. Lord knew he'd thought about doing this with Olive so many times, but now it was actually happening, and the reality was so much better than any of his fantasies.

She ground against him, making his hard cock ache to be inside her, but some small shred of common sense still niggled in the back of his mind, making him say, "I won't be in town long. And I don't have a condom with me."

"I know you aren't staying," she said, reaching her fingers down to tickle his sensitive balls and making him groan low in his throat. "It's fine. I want you, I want this. One night is enough. And I'm on the pill, don't worry."

Levon kissed her hard and deep, pulling back as she rose up to position him at her wet entrance. Those warning bells went off in his head again before he shut them off. Something was wrong here, but his mind was too fuzzy to think of what.

You need to be inside her, that's what's wrong.

Then Olive sank down onto his hard cock, her warm, wet, tight channel fitting him like a glove, and any last remnants of coherent thought left him completely. "Oh God, Olive. You feel amazing."

She leaned in, trailing kisses down his neck as she rode him to her pleasure. "So do you. So, so good."

Then there was no more talk, just kisses and caresses and moans of ecstasy as the truck windows steamed up and they both got pulled under by a riptide of desire.

Grab your copy of *Protecting His Pregnant Lover* (Southern Soldiers of Fortune Book One) from www.LeslieNorthBooks.com

www.ingramcontent.com/pod-product-compliance
Lightning Source LLC
Chambersburg PA
CBHW071935150726
47999CB00001B/214